HENRY V

(HENRY THE FIFTH)

BY WILLIAM SHAKESPEARE

CONTENTS

Prologue

O For a Muse of Fire, that would ascend
The brightest Heauen of Inuention:
A Kingdome for a Stage, Princes to Act,
And Monarchs to behold the swelling Scene.
Then should the Warlike Harry, like himselfe,
Assume the Port of Mars, and at his heeles
(Leasht in, like Hounds) should Famine, Sword, and Fire
Crouch for employment. But pardon, Gentles all:
The flat vnraysed Spirits, that hath dar'd,
On this vnworthy Scaffold, to bring forth
So great an Obiect. Can this Cock-Pit hold
The vastie fields of France? Or may we cramme
Within this Woodden O, the very Caskes
That did affright the Ayre at Agincourt?
O pardon: since a crooked Figure may
Attest in little place a Million,
And let vs, Cyphers to this great Accompt,
On your imaginarie Forces worke.
Suppose within the Girdle of these Walls
Are now confin'd two mightie Monarchies,
Whose high, vp-reared, and abutting Fronts,
The perillous narrow Ocean parts asunder.
Peece out our imperfections with your thoughts:
Into a thousand parts diuide one Man,
And make imaginarie Puissance.
Thinke when we talke of Horses, that you see them
Printing their prowd Hoofes i'th' receiuing Earth:
For 'tis your thoughts that now must deck our Kings,
Carry them here and there: Iumping o're Times;
Turning th' accomplishment of many yeeres
Into an Howre-glasse: for the which supplie,
Admit me Chorus to this Historie;
Who Prologue-like, your humble patience pray,
Gently to heare, kindly to iudge our Play.

Actus Primus.

Scoena Prima.

Enter the two Bishops of Canterbury and Ely.

Bish.Cant. My Lord, Ile tell you, that selfe Bill is vrg'd,
Which in th' eleue[n]th yere of y last Kings reign
Was like, and had indeed against vs past,
But that the scambling and vnquiet time
Did push it out of farther question

Bish.Ely. But how my Lord shall we resist it now?

Bish.Cant. It must be thought on: if it passe against vs,
We loose the better halfe of our Possession:
For all the Temporall Lands, which men deuout
By Testament haue giuen to the Church,
Would they strip from vs; being valu'd thus,
As much as would maintaine, to the Kings honor,
Full fifteene Earles, and fifteene hundred Knights,
Six thousand and two hundred good Esquires:
And to reliefe of Lazars, and weake age
Of indigent faint Soules, past corporall toyle,
A hundred Almes-houses, right well supply'd:
And to the Coffers of the King beside,
A thousand pounds by th' yeere. Thus runs the Bill

Bish.Ely. This would drinke deepe

Bish.Cant. 'Twould drinke the Cup and all

Bish.Ely. But what preuention?

Bish.Cant. The King is full of grace, and faire regard

Bish.Ely. And a true louer of the holy Church

Bish.Cant. The courses of his youth promis'd it not.
The breath no sooner left his Fathers body,
But that his wildnesse, mortify'd in him,
Seem'd to dye too: yea, at that very moment,
Consideration like an Angell came,
And whipt th' offending Adam out of him;
Leauing his body as a Paradise,
T' inuelop and containe Celestiall Spirits.
Neuer was such a sodaine Scholler made:
Neuer came Reformation in a Flood,
With such a heady currance scowring faults:
Nor neuer Hidra-headed Wilfulnesse
So soone did loose his Seat; and all at once;
As in this King

Bish.Ely. We are blessed in the Change

Bish.Cant. Heare him but reason in Diuinitie;
And all-admiring, with an inward wish
You would desire the King were made a Prelate:
Heare him debate of Common-wealth Affaires;
You would say, it hath been all in all his study:
List his discourse of Warre; and you shall heare
A fearefull Battaile rendred you in Musique.
Turne him to any Cause of Pollicy,
The Gordian Knot of it he will vnloose,
Familiar as his Garter: that when he speakes,
The Ayre, a Charter'd Libertine, is still,
And the mute Wonder lurketh in mens eares,
To steale his sweet and honyed Sentences:
So that the Art and Practique part of Life,
Must be the Mistresse to this Theorique.
Which is a wonder how his Grace should gleane it,
Since his addiction was to Courses vaine,
His Companies vnletter'd, rude, and shallow,

His Houres fill'd vp with Ryots, Banquets, Sports;
And neuer noted in him any studie,
Any retyrement, any sequestration,
From open Haunts and Popularitie

B.Ely. The Strawberry growes vnderneath the Nettle,
And holesome Berryes thriue and ripen best,
Neighbour'd by Fruit of baser qualitie:
And so the Prince obscur'd his Contemplation
Vnder the Veyle of Wildnesse, which (no doubt)
Grew like the Summer Grasse, fastest by Night,
Vnseene, yet cressiue in his facultie

B.Cant. It must be so; for Miracles are ceast:
And therefore we must needes admit the meanes,
How things are perfected

B.Ely. But my good Lord:
How now for mittigation of this Bill,
Vrg'd by the Commons? doth his Maiestie
Incline to it, or no?
B.Cant. He seemes indifferent:
Or rather swaying more vpon our part,
Then cherishing th' exhibiters against vs:
For I haue made an offer to his Maiestie,
Vpon our Spirituall Conuocation,
And in regard of Causes now in hand,
Which I haue open'd to his Grace at large,
As touching France, to giue a greater Summe,
Then euer at one time the Clergie yet
Did to his Predecessors part withall

B.Ely. How did this offer seeme receiu'd, my Lord?
B.Cant. With good acceptance of his Maiestie:
Saue that there was not time enough to heare,
As I perceiu'd his Grace would faine haue done,
The seueralls and vnhidden passages

3

Of his true Titles to some certaine Dukedomes,
And generally, to the Crowne and Seat of France,
Deriu'd from Edward, his great Grandfather

B.Ely. What was th' impediment that broke this off?
B.Cant. The French Embassador vpon that instant
Crau'd audience; and the howre I thinke is come,
To giue him hearing: Is it foure a Clock?
B.Ely. It is

B.Cant. Then goe we in, to know his Embassie:
Which I could with a ready guesse declare,
Before the Frenchman speake a word of it

B.Ely. Ile wait vpon you, and I long to heare it.

Exeunt.

Enter the King, Humfrey, Bedford, Clarence, Warwick,
Westmerland, and
Exeter.

King. Where is my gracious Lord of Canterbury?
Exeter. Not here in presence

King. Send for him, good Vnckle

Westm. Shall we call in th' Ambassador, my Liege?
King. Not yet, my Cousin: we would be resolu'd,
Before we heare him, of some things of weight,
That taske our thoughts, concerning vs and France.
Enter two Bishops.

B.Cant. God and his Angels guard your sacred Throne,
And make you long become it

King. Sure we thanke you.

4

My learned Lord, we pray you to proceed,
And iustly and religiously vnfold,
Why the Law Salike, that they haue in France,
Or should or should not barre vs in our Clayme:
And God forbid, my deare and faithfull Lord,
That you should fashion, wrest, or bow your reading,
Or nicely charge your vnderstanding Soule,
With opening Titles miscreate, whose right
Sutes not in natiue colours with the truth:
For God doth know, how many now in health,
Shall drop their blood, in approbation
Of what your reuerence shall incite vs to.
Therefore take heed how you impawne our Person,
How you awake our sleeping Sword of Warre;
We charge you in the Name of God take heed:
For neuer two such Kingdomes did contend,
Without much fall of blood, whose guiltlesse drops
Are euery one, a Woe, a sore Complaint,
'Gainst him, whose wrongs giues edge vnto the Swords,
That makes such waste in briefe mortalitie.
Vnder this Coniuration, speake my Lord:
For we will heare, note, and beleeue in heart,
That what you speake, is in your Conscience washt,
As pure as sinne with Baptisme

B.Can. Then heare me gracious Soueraign, & you Peers,
That owe your selues, your liues, and seruices,
To this Imperiall Throne. There is no barre
To make against your Highnesse Clayme to France,
But this which they produce from Pharamond,
In terram Salicam Mulieres ne succedant,
No Woman shall succeed in Salike Land:
Which Salike Land, the French vniustly gloze
To be the Realme of France, and Pharamond
The founder of this Law, and Female Barre.
Yet their owne Authors faithfully affirme,
That the Land Salike is in Germanie,

Betweene the Flouds of Sala and of Elue:
Where Charles the Great hauing subdu'd the Saxons,
There left behind and settled certaine French:
Who holding in disdaine the German Women,
For some dishonest manners of their life,
Establisht then this Law; to wit, No Female
Should be Inheritrix in Salike Land:
Which Salike (as I said) 'twixt Elue and Sala,
Is at this day in Germanie, call'd Meisen.
Then doth it well appeare, the Salike Law
Was not deuised for the Realme of France:
Nor did the French possesse the Salike Land,
Vntill foure hundred one and twentie yeeres
After defunction of King Pharamond,
Idly suppos'd the founder of this Law,
Who died within the yeere of our Redemption,
Foure hundred twentie six: and Charles the Great
Subdu'd the Saxons, and did seat the French
Beyond the Riuer Sala, in the yeere
Eight hundred fiue. Besides, their Writers say,
King Pepin, which deposed Childerike,
Did as Heire Generall, being descended
Of Blithild, which was Daughter to King Clothair,
Make Clayme and Title to the Crowne of France.
Hugh Capet also, who vsurpt the Crowne
Of Charles the Duke of Loraine, sole Heire male
Of the true Line and Stock of Charles the Great:
To find his Title with some shewes of truth,
Though in pure truth it was corrupt and naught,
Conuey'd himselfe as th' Heire to th' Lady Lingare,
Daughter to Charlemaine, who was the Sonne
To Lewes the Emperour, and Lewes the Sonne
Of Charles the Great: also King Lewes the Tenth,
Who was sole Heire to the Vsurper Capet,
Could not keepe quiet in his conscience,
Wearing the Crowne of France, 'till satisfied,
That faire Queene Isabel, his Grandmother,

Was Lineall of the Lady Ermengare,
Daughter to Charles the foresaid Duke of Loraine:
By the which Marriage, the Lyne of Charles the Great
Was re-vnited to the Crowne of France.
So, that as cleare as is the Summers Sunne,
King Pepins Title, and Hugh Capets Clayme,
King Lewes his satisfaction, all appeare
To hold in Right and Title of the Female:
So doe the Kings of France vnto this day.
Howbeit, they would hold vp this Salique Law,
To barre your Highnesse clayming from the Female,
And rather chuse to hide them in a Net,
Then amply to imbarre their crooked Titles,
Vsurpt from you and your Progenitors

King. May I with right and conscience make this claim?
Bish.Cant. The sinne vpon my head, dread Soueraigne:
For in the Booke of Numbers is it writ,
When the man dyes, let the Inheritance
Descend vnto the Daughter. Gracious Lord,
Stand for your owne, vnwind your bloody Flagge,
Looke back into your mightie Ancestors:
Goe my dread Lord, to your great Grandsires Tombe,
From whom you clayme; inuoke his Warlike Spirit,
And your Great Vnckles, Edward the Black Prince,
Who on the French ground play'd a Tragedie,
Making defeat on the full Power of France:
Whiles his most mightie Father on a Hill
Stood smiling, to behold his Lyons Whelpe
Forrage in blood of French Nobilitie.
O Noble English, that could entertaine
With halfe their Forces, the full pride of France,
And let another halfe stand laughing by,
All out of worke, and cold for action

Bish. Awake remembrance of these valiant dead,
And with your puissant Arme renew their Feats;

You are their Heire, you sit vpon their Throne:
The Blood and Courage that renowned them,
Runs in your Veines: and my thrice-puissant Liege
Is in the very May-Morne of his Youth,
Ripe for Exploits and mightie Enterprises

Exe. Your Brother Kings and Monarchs of the Earth
Doe all expect, that you should rowse your selfe,
As did the former Lyons of your Blood

West. They know your Grace hath cause, and means, and might;
So hath your Highnesse: neuer King of England
Had Nobles richer, and more loyall Subiects,
Whose hearts haue left their bodyes here in England,
And lye pauillion'd in the fields of France

Bish.Can. O let their bodyes follow my deare Liege
With Bloods, and Sword and Fire, to win your Right:
In ayde whereof, we of the Spiritualtie
Will rayse your Highnesse such a mightie Summe,
As neuer did the Clergie at one time
Bring in to any of your Ancestors

King. We must not onely arme t' inuade the French,
But lay downe our proportions, to defend
Against the Scot, who will make roade vpon vs,
With all aduantages

Bish.Can. They of those Marches, gracious Soueraign,
Shall be a Wall sufficient to defend
Our in-land from the pilfering Borderers

King. We do not meane the coursing snatchers onely,
But feare the maine intendment of the Scot,
Who hath been still a giddy neighbour to vs:
For you shall reade, that my great Grandfather
Neuer went with his forces into France,

But that the Scot, on his vnfurnisht Kingdome,
Came pouring like the Tyde into a breach,
With ample and brim fulnesse of his force,
Galling the gleaned Land with hot Assayes,
Girding with grieuous siege, Castles and Townes:
That England being emptie of defence,
Hath shooke and trembled at th' ill neighbourhood

B.Can. She hath bin the[n] more fear'd the[n] harm'd, my Liege:
For heare her but exampl'd by her selfe,
When all her Cheualrie hath been in France,
And shee a mourning Widdow of her Nobles,
Shee hath her selfe not onely well defended,
But taken and impounded as a Stray,
The King of Scots: whom shee did send to France,
To fill King Edwards fame with prisoner Kings,
And make their Chronicle as rich with prayse,
As is the Owse and bottome of the Sea
With sunken Wrack, and sum-lesse Treasuries

Bish.Ely. But there's a saying very old and true,
If that you will France win, then with Scotland first begin.
For once the Eagle (England) being in prey,
To her vnguarded Nest, the Weazell (Scot)
Comes sneaking, and so sucks her Princely Egges,
Playing the Mouse in absence of the Cat,
To tame and hauocke more then she can eate

Exet. It followes then, the Cat must stay at home,
Yet that is but a crush'd necessity,
Since we haue lockes to safegard necessaries,
And pretty traps to catch the petty theeues.
While that the Armed hand doth fight abroad,
Th' aduised head defends it selfe at home:
For Gouernment, though high, and low, and lower,
Put into parts, doth keepe in one consent,
Congreeing in a full and natural close,

9

Like Musicke

Cant. Therefore doth heauen diuide
The state of man in diuers functions,
Setting endeuour in continual motion:
To which is fixed as an ayme or butt,
Obedience: for so worke the Hony Bees,
Creatures that by a rule in Nature teach
The Act of Order to a peopled Kingdome.
They haue a King, and Officers of sorts,
Where some like Magistrates correct at home:
Others, like Merchants venter Trade abroad:
Others, like Souldiers armed in their stings,
Make boote vpon the Summers Veluet buddes:
Which pillage, they with merry march bring home
To the Tent-royal of their Emperor:
Who busied in his Maiesties surueyes
The singing Masons building roofes of Gold,
The ciuil Citizens kneading vp the hony;
The poore Mechanicke Porters, crowding in
Their heauy burthens at his narrow gate:
The sad-ey'd Iustice with his surly humme,
Deliuering ore to Executors pale
The lazie yawning Drone: I this inferre,
That many things hauing full reference
To one consent, may worke contrariously,
As many Arrowes loosed seuerall wayes
Come to one marke: as many wayes meet in one towne,
As many fresh streames meet in one salt sea;
As many Lynes close in the Dials center:
So may a thousand actions once a foote,
And in one purpose, and be all well borne
Without defeat. Therefore to France, my Liege,
Diuide your happy England into foure,
Whereof, take you one quarter into France,
And you withall shall make all Gallia shake.
If we with thrice such powers left at home,

Cannot defend our owne doores from the dogge,
Let vs be worried, and our Nation lose
The name of hardinesse and policie

King. Call in the Messengers sent from the Dolphin.
Now are we well resolu'd, and by Gods helpe
And yours, the noble sinewes of our power,
France being ours, wee'l bend it to our Awe,
Or breake it all to peeces. Or there wee'l sit,
(Ruling in large and ample Emperie,
Ore France, and all her (almost) Kingly Dukedomes)
Or lay these bones in an vnworthy Vrne,
Tomblesse, with no remembrance ouer them:
Either our History shall with full mouth
Speake freely of our Acts, or else our graue
Like Turkish mute, shall haue a tonguelesse mouth,
Not worshipt with a waxen Epitaph.
Enter Ambassadors of France.

Now are we well prepar'd to know the pleasure
Of our faire Cosin Dolphin: for we heare,
Your greeting is from him, not from the King

Amb. May't please your Maiestie to giue vs leaue
Freely to render what we haue in charge:
Or shall we sparingly shew you farre off
The Dolphins meaning, and our Embassie

King. We are no Tyrant, but a Christian King,
Vnto whose grace our passion is as subiect
As is our wretches fettred in our prisons,
Therefore with franke and with vncurbed plainnesse,
Tell vs the Dolphins minde

Amb. Thus than in few:
Your Highnesse lately sending into France,
Did claime some certaine Dukedomes, in the right

Of your great Predecessor, King Edward the third.
In answer of which claime, the Prince our Master
Sayes, that you sauour too much of your youth,
And bids you be aduis'd: There's nought in France,
That can be with a nimble Galliard wonne:
You cannot reuell into Dukedomes there.
He therefore sends you meeter for your spirit
This Tun of Treasure; and in lieu of this,
Desires you let the dukedomes that you claime
Heare no more of you. This the Dolphin speakes

King. What Treasure Vncle?
Exe. Tennis balles, my Liege

Kin. We are glad the Dolphin is so pleasant with vs,
His Present, and your paines we thanke you for:
When we haue matcht our Rackets to these Balles,
We will in France (by Gods grace) play a set,
Shall strike his fathers Crowne into the hazard.
Tell him, he hath made a match with such a Wrangler,
That all the Courts of France will be disturb'd
With Chaces. And we vnderstand him well,
How he comes o're vs with our wilder dayes,
Not measuring what vse we made of them.
We neuer valew'd this poore seate of England,
And therefore liuing hence, did giue our selfe
To barbarous license: As 'tis euer common,
That men are merriest, when they are from home.
But tell the Dolphin, I will keepe my State,
Be like a King, and shew my sayle of Greatnesse,
When I do rowse me in my Throne of France.
For that I haue layd by my Maiestie,
And plodded like a man for working dayes:
But I will rise there with so full a glorie,
That I will dazle all the eyes of France,
Yea strike the Dolphin blinde to looke on vs,
And tell the pleasant Prince, this Mocke of his

Hath turn'd his balles to Gun-stones, and his soule
Shall stand sore charged, for the wastefull vengeance
That shall flye with them: for many a thousand widows
Shall this his Mocke, mocke out of their deer husbands;
Mocke mothers from their sonnes, mock Castles downe:
And some are yet vngotten and vnborne,
That shal haue cause to curse the Dolphins scorne.
But this lyes all within the wil of God,
To whom I do appeale, and in whose name
Tel you the Dolphin, I am comming on,
To venge me as I may, and to put forth
My rightfull hand in a wel-hallow'd cause.
So get you hence in peace: And tell the Dolphin,
His Iest will sauour but of shallow wit,
When thousands weepe more then did laugh at it.
Conuey them with safe conduct. Fare you well.

Exeunt. Ambassadors.

Exe. This was a merry Message

King. We hope to make the Sender blush at it:
Therefore, my Lords, omit no happy howre,
That may giue furth'rance to our Expedition:
For we haue now no thought in vs but France,
Saue those to God, that runne before our businesse.
Therefore let our proportions for these Warres
Be soone collected, and all things thought vpon,
That may with reasonable swiftnesse adde
More Feathers to our Wings: for God before,
Wee'le chide this Dolphin at his fathers doore.
Therefore let euery man now taske his thought,
That this faire Action may on foot be brought.

Exeunt.

Flourish. Enter Chorus.

Now all the Youth of England are on fire,
And silken Dalliance in the Wardrobe lyes:
Now thriue the Armorers, and Honors thought
Reignes solely in the breast of euery man.
They sell the Pasture now, to buy the Horse;
Following the Mirror of all Christian Kings,
With winged heeles, as English Mercuries.
For now sits Expectation in the Ayre,
And hides a Sword, from Hilts vnto the Point,
With Crownes Imperiall, Crownes and Coronets,
Promis'd to Harry, and his followers.
The French aduis'd by good intelligence
Of this most dreadfull preparation,
Shake in their feare, and with pale Pollicy
Seeke to diuert the English purposes.
O England: Modell to thy inward Greatnesse,
Like little Body with a mightie Heart:
What mightst thou do, that honour would thee do,
Were all thy children kinde and naturall:
But see, thy fault France hath in thee found out,
A nest of hollow bosomes, which he filles
With treacherous Crownes, and three corrupted men:
One, Richard Earle of Cambridge, and the second
Henry Lord Scroope of Masham, and the third
Sir Thomas Grey Knight of Northumberland,
Haue for the Gilt of France (O guilt indeed)
Confirm'd Conspiracy with fearefull France,
And by their hands, this grace of Kings must dye.
If Hell and Treason hold their promises,
Ere he take ship for France; and in Southampton.
Linger your patience on, and wee'l digest
Th' abuse of distance; force a play:
The summe is payde, the Traitors are agreed,
The King is set from London, and the Scene
Is now transported (Gentles) to Southampton,
There is the Play-house now, there must you sit,

And thence to France shall we conuey you safe,
And bring you backe: Charming the narrow seas
To giue you gentle Passe: for if we may,
Wee'l not offend one stomacke with our Play.
But till the King come forth, and not till then,
Vnto Southampton do we shift our Scene.

Exit

Enter Corporall Nym, and Lieutenant Bardolfe.

Bar. Well met Corporall Nym

Nym. Good morrow Lieutenant Bardolfe

Bar. What, are Ancient Pistoll and you friends yet? Nym. For my
part, I care not: I say little: but when time shall serue, there shall
be smiles, but that shall be as it may. I dare not fight, but I will
winke and holde out mine yron: it is a simple one, but what
though? It will toste Cheese, and it will endure cold, as another
mans sword will: and there's an end

Bar. I will bestow a breakfast to make you friendes, and wee'l bee
all three sworne brothers to France: Let't be so good Corporall
Nym

Nym. Faith, I will liue so long as I may, that's the certaine of it:
and when I cannot liue any longer, I will doe as I may: That is
my rest, that is the rendeuous of it

Bar. It is certaine Corporall, that he is marryed to Nell Quickly,
and certainly she did you wrong, for you were troth-plight to her

Nym. I cannot tell, Things must be as they may: men may sleepe,
and they may haue their throats about them at that time, and
some say, kniues haue edges: It must be as it may, though

patience be a tyred name, yet shee will plodde, there must be
Conclusions, well, I cannot tell. Enter Pistoll, & Quickly.

Bar. Heere comes Ancient Pistoll and his wife: good
Corporall be patient heere. How now mine Hoaste Pistoll?
Pist. Base Tyke, cal'st thou mee Hoste, now by this
hand I sweare I scorne the terme: nor shall my Nel keep
Lodgers

Host. No by my troth, not long: For we cannot lodge and board a
dozen or fourteene Gentlewomen that liue honestly by the pricke
of their Needles, but it will bee thought we keepe a Bawdy-house
straight. O welliday Lady, if he be not hewne now, we shall see
wilful adultery and murther committed

Bar. Good Lieutenant, good Corporal offer nothing heere

Nym. Pish

Pist. Pish for thee, Island dogge: thou prickeard cur
of Island

Host. Good Corporall Nym shew thy valor, and put
vp your sword

Nym. Will you shogge off? I would haue you solus

Pist. Solus, egregious dog? O Viper vile; The solus in thy most
meruailous face, the solus in thy teeth, and in thy throate, and in
thy hatefull Lungs, yea in thy Maw perdy; and which is worse,
within thy nastie mouth. I do retort the solus in thy bowels, for I
can take, and Pistols cocke is vp, and flashing fire will follow

Nym. I am not Barbason, you cannot coniure mee: I haue an
humor to knocke you indifferently well: If you grow fowle with
me Pistoll, I will scoure you with my Rapier, as I may, in fayre

tearmes. If you would walke off, I would pricke your guts a little in good tearmes, as I may, and that's the humor of it

Pist. O Braggard vile, and damned furious wight,
The Graue doth gape, and doting death is neere,
Therefore exhale

Bar. Heare me, heare me what I say: Hee that strikes
the first stroake, Ile run him vp to the hilts, as I am a soldier

Pist. An oath of mickle might, and fury shall abate. Giue me thy
fist, thy fore-foote to me giue: Thy spirites are most tall

Nym. I will cut thy throate one time or other in faire
termes, that is the humor of it

Pistoll. Couple a gorge, that is the word. I defie thee againe.
O hound of Creet, think'st thou my spouse to get?
No, to the spittle goe, and from the Poudring tub of infamy,
fetch forth the Lazar Kite of Cressids kinde, Doll
Teare-sheete, she by name, and her espouse. I haue, and I
will hold the Quondam Quickely for the onely shee: and
Pauca, there's enough to go to.
Enter the Boy.

Boy. Mine Hoast Pistoll, you must come to my Mayster, and your
Hostesse: He is very sicke, & would to bed. Good Bardolfe, put
thy face betweene his sheets, and do the Office of a Warming-
pan: Faith, he's very ill

Bard. Away you Rogue

Host. By my troth he'l yeeld the Crow a pudding one of these
dayes: the King has kild his heart. Good Husband come home
presently.

Exit

Bar. Come, shall I make you two friends. Wee must to France together: why the diuel should we keep kniues to cut one anothers throats? Pist. Let floods ore-swell, and fiends for food howle on

Nym. You'l pay me the eight shillings I won of you at Betting?
Pist. Base is the Slaue that payes

Nym. That now I wil haue: that's the humor of it

Pist. As manhood shal compound: push home.

Draw

Bard. By this sword, hee that makes the first thrust, Ile kill him: By this sword, I wil

Pi. Sword is an Oath, & Oaths must haue their course
Bar. Coporall Nym, & thou wilt be friends be frends, and thou wilt not, why then be enemies with me to: prethee put vp

Pist. A Noble shalt thou haue, and present pay, and Liquor likewise will I giue to thee, and friendshippe shall combyne, and brotherhood. Ile liue by Nymme, & Nymme shall liue by me, is not this iust? For I shal Sutler be vnto the Campe, and profits will accrue. Giue mee thy hand

Nym. I shall haue my Noble?
Pist. In cash, most iustly payd

Nym. Well, then that the humor of't.
Enter Hostesse.

18

Host. As euer you come of women, come in quickly to sir Iohn: A
poore heart, hee is so shak'd of a burning quotidian Tertian, that
it is most lamentable to behold. Sweet men, come to him

Nym. The King hath run bad humors on the Knight,
that's the euen of it

Pist. Nym, thou hast spoke the right, his heart is fracted
and corroborate

Nym. The King is a good King, but it must bee as it
may: he passes some humors, and carreeres

Pist. Let vs condole the Knight, for (Lambekins) we
will liue.
Enter Exeter, Bedford, & Westmerland.

Bed. Fore God his Grace is bold to trust these traitors
Exe. They shall be apprehended by and by

West. How smooth and euen they do bear themselues,
As if allegeance in their bosomes sate
Crowned with faith, and constant loyalty

Bed. The King hath note of all that they intend,
By interception, which they dreame not of

Exe. Nay, but the man that was his bedfellow,
Whom he hath dull'd and cloy'd with gracious fauours;
That he should for a forraigne purse, so sell
His Soueraignes life to death and treachery.

Sound Trumpets.

Enter the King, Scroope, Cambridge, and Gray.

King. Now sits the winde faire, and we will aboord.

19

My Lord of Cambridge, and my kinde Lord of Masham,
And you my gentle Knight, giue me your thoughts:
Thinke you not that the powres we beare with vs
Will cut their passage through the force of France?
Doing the execution, and the acte,
For which we haue in head assembled them

Scro. No doubt my Liege, if each man do his best

King. I doubt not that, since we are well perswaded
We carry not a heart with vs from hence,
That growes not in a faire consent with ours:
Nor leaue not one behinde, that doth not wish
Successe and Conquest to attend on vs

Cam. Neuer was Monarch better fear'd and lou'd,
Then is your Maiesty; there's not I thinke a subiect
That sits in heart-greefe and vneasinesse
Vnder the sweet shade of your gouernment

Kni. True: those that were your Fathers enemies,
Haue steep'd their gauls in hony, and do serue you
With hearts create of duty, and of zeale

King. We therefore haue great cause of thankfulnes,
And shall forget the office of our hand
Sooner then quittance of desert and merit,
According to the weight and worthinesse

Scro. So seruice shall with steeled sinewes toyle,
And labour shall refresh it selfe with hope
To do your Grace incessant seruices

King. We Iudge no lesse. Vnkle of Exeter,
Inlarge the man committed yesterday,
That rayl'd against our person: We consider
It was excesse of Wine that set him on,

And on his more aduice, We pardon him

Scro. That's mercy, but too much security:
Let him be punish'd Soueraigne, least example
Breed (by his sufferance) more of such a kind

King. O let vs yet be mercifull

Cam. So may your Highnesse, and yet punish too

Grey. Sir, you shew great mercy if you giue him life,
After the taste of much correction

King. Alas, your too much loue and care of me,
Are heauy Orisons 'gainst this poore wretch:
If little faults proceeding on distemper,
Shall not be wink'd at, how shall we stretch our eye
When capitall crimes, chew'd, swallow'd, and digested,
Appeare before vs? Wee'l yet inlarge that man,
Though Cambridge, Scroope, and Gray, in their deere care
And tender preseruation of our person
Wold haue him punish'd. And now to our French causes,
Who are the late Commissioners?
Cam. I one my Lord,
Your Highnesse bad me aske for it to day

Scro. So did you me my Liege

Gray. And I my Royall Soueraigne

King. Then Richard Earle of Cambridge, there is yours:
There yours Lord Scroope of Masham, and Sir Knight:
Gray of Northumberland, this same is yours:
Reade them, and know I know your worthinesse.
My Lord of Westmerland, and Vnkle Exeter,
We will aboord to night. Why how now Gentlemen?
What see you in those papers, that you loose

So much complexion? Looke ye how they change:
Their cheekes are paper. Why, what reade you there,
That haue so cowarded and chac'd your blood
Out of apparance

Cam. I do confesse my fault,
And do submit me to your Highnesse mercy

Gray. Scro. To which we all appeale

King. The mercy that was quicke in vs but late,
By your owne counsaile is supprest and kill'd:
You must not dare (for shame) to talke of mercy,
For your owne reasons turne into your bosomes,
As dogs vpon their maisters, worrying you:
See you my Princes, and my Noble Peeres,
These English monsters: My Lord of Cambridge heere,
You know how apt our loue was, to accord
To furnish with all appertinents
Belonging to his Honour; and this man,
Hath for a few light Crownes, lightly conspir'd
And sworne vnto the practises of France
To kill vs heere in Hampton. To the which,
This Knight no lesse for bounty bound to Vs
Then Cambridge is, hath likewise sworne. But O,
What shall I say to thee Lord Scroope, thou cruell,
Ingratefull, sauage, and inhumane Creature?
Thou that didst beare the key of all my counsailes,
That knew'st the very bottome of my soule,
That (almost) might'st haue coyn'd me into Golde,
Would'st thou haue practis'd on me, for thy vse?
May it be possible, that forraigne hyer
Could out of thee extract one sparke of euill
That might annoy my finger? 'Tis so strange,
That though the truth of it stands off as grosse
As black and white, my eye will scarsely see it.
Treason, and murther, euer kept together,

As two yoake diuels sworne to eythers purpose,
Working so grossely in an naturall cause,
That admiration did not hoope at them.
But thou (gainst all proportion) didst bring in
Wonder to waite on treason, and on murther:
And whatsoeuer cunning fiend it was
That wrought vpon thee so preposterously,
Hath got the voyce in hell for excellence:
And other diuels that suggest by treasons,
Do botch and bungle vp damnation,
With patches, colours, and with formes being fetcht
From glist'ring semblances of piety:
But he that temper'd thee, bad thee stand vp,
Gaue thee no instance why thou shouldst do treason,
Vnlesse to dub thee with the name of Traitor.
If that same Daemon that hath gull'd thee thus,
Should with his Lyon-gate walke the whole world,
He might returne to vastie Tartar backe,
And tell the Legions, I can neuer win
A soule so easie as that Englishmans.
Oh, how hast thou with iealousie infected
The sweetnesse of affiance? Shew men dutifull,
Why so didst thou: seeme they graue and learned?
Why so didst thou. Come they of Noble Family?
Why so didst thou. Seeme they religious?
Why so didst thou. Or are they spare in diet,
Free from grosse passion, or of mirth, or anger,
Constant in spirit, not sweruing with the blood,
Garnish'd and deck'd in modest complement,
Not working with the eye, without the eare,
And but in purged iudgement trusting neither,
Such and so finely boulted didst thou seeme:
And thus thy fall hath left a kinde of blot,
To make thee full fraught man, and best indued
With some suspition, I will weepe for thee.
For this reuolt of thine, me thinkes is like
Another fall of Man. Their faults are open,

Arrest them to the answer of the Law,
And God acquit them of their practises

Exe. I arrest thee of High Treason, by the name of
Richard Earle of Cambridge.
I arrest thee of High Treason, by the name of Thomas
Lord Scroope of Marsham.
I arrest thee of High Treason, by the name of Thomas
Grey, Knight of Northumberland

Scro. Our purposes, God iustly hath discouer'd,
And I repent my fault more then my death,
Which I beseech your Highnesse to forgiue,
Although my body pay the price of it

Cam. For me, the Gold of France did not seduce,
Although I did admit it as a motiue,
The sooner to effect what I intended:
But God be thanked for preuention,
Which in sufferance heartily will reioyce,
Beseeching God, and you, to pardon mee

Gray. Neuer did faithfull subiect more reioyce
At the discouery of most dangerous Treason,
Then I do at this houre ioy ore my selfe,
Preuented from a damned enterprize;
My fault, but not my body, pardon Soueraigne

King. God quit you in his mercy: Hear your sentence
You haue conspir'd against Our Royall person,
Ioyn'd with an enemy proclaim'd, and from his Coffers,
Receyu'd the Golden Earnest of Our death:
Wherein you would haue sold your King to slaughter,
His Princes, and his Peeres to seruitude,
His Subiects to oppression, and contempt,
And his whole Kingdome into desolation:
Touching our person, seeke we no reuenge,

But we our Kingdomes safety must so tender,
Whose ruine you sought, that to her Lawes
We do deliuer you. Get you therefore hence,
(Poore miserable wretches) to your death:
The taste whereof, God of his mercy giue
You patience to indure, and true Repentance
Of all your deare offences. Beare them hence.
Enter.

Now Lords for France: the enterprise whereof
Shall be to you as vs, like glorious.
We doubt not of a faire and luckie Warre,
Since God so graciously hath brought to light
This dangerous Treason, lurking in our way,
To hinder our beginnings. We doubt not now,
But euery Rubbe is smoothed on our way.
Then forth, deare Countreymen: Let vs deliuer
Our Puissance into the hand of God,
Putting it straight in expedition.
Chearely to Sea, the signes of Warre aduance,
No King of England, if not King of France.

Flourish.

Enter Pistoll, Nim, Bardolph, Boy, and Hostesse.

Hostesse. 'Prythee honey sweet Husband, let me bring thee to
Staines

Pistoll. No: for my manly heart doth erne. Bardolph, be blythe:
Nim, rowse thy vaunting Veines: Boy, brissle thy Courage vp: for
Falstaffe hee is dead, and wee must erne therefore

Bard. Would I were with him, wheresomere hee is, eyther in
Heauen, or in Hell

Hostesse. Nay sure, hee's not in Hell: hee's in Arthurs Bosome, if euer man went to Arthurs Bosome: a made a finer end, and went away and it had beene any Christome Childe: a parted eu'n iust betweene Twelue and One, eu'n at the turning o'th' Tyde: for after I saw him fumble with the Sheets, and play with Flowers, and smile vpon his fingers end, I knew there was but one way: for his Nose was as sharpe as a Pen, and a Table of greene fields. How now Sir Iohn (quoth I?) what man? be a good cheare: so a cryed out, God, God, God, three or foure times: now I, to comfort him, bid him a should not thinke of God; I hop'd there was no neede to trouble himselfe with any such thoughts yet: so a bad me lay more Clothes on his feet: I put my hand into the Bed, and felt them, and they were as cold as any stone: then I felt to his knees, and so vp-peer'd, and vpward, and all was as cold as any stone

Nim. They say he cryed out of Sack

Hostesse. I, that a did

Bard. And of Women

Hostesse. Nay, that a did not

Boy. Yes that a did, and said they were Deules incarnate

Woman. A could neuer abide Carnation, 'twas a Colour
he neuer lik'd

Boy. A said once, the Deule would haue him about
Women

Hostesse. A did in some sort (indeed) handle Women: but then
hee was rumatique, and talk'd of the Whore of Babylon

Boy. Doe you not remember a saw a Flea sticke vpon Bardolphs
Nose, and a said it was a blacke Soule burning in Hell

Bard. Well, the fuell is gone that maintain'd that fire: that's all the Riches I got in his seruice

Nim. Shall wee shogg? the King will be gone from Southampton

Pist. Come, let's away. My Loue, giue me thy Lippes: Looke to my Chattels, and my Moueables: Let Sences rule: The world is, Pitch and pay: trust none: for Oathes are Strawes, mens Faiths are Wafer-Cakes, and hold-fast is the onely Dogge: My Ducke, therefore Caueto bee thy Counsailor. Goe, cleare thy Chrystalls. Yokefellowes in Armes, let vs to France, like Horseleeches my Boyes, to sucke, to sucke, the very blood to sucke

Boy. And that's but vnwholesome food, they say

Pist. Touch her soft mouth, and march

Bard. Farwell Hostesse

Nim. I cannot kisse, that is the humor of it: but adieu

Pist. Let Huswiferie appeare: keepe close, I thee command

Hostesse. Farwell: adieu.

Exeunt.

Flourish.

Enter the French King, the Dolphin, the Dukes of Berry and Britaine.

King. Thus comes the English with full power vpon vs,

And more then carefully it vs concernes,
To answer Royally in our defences.
Therefore the Dukes of Berry and of Britaine,
Of Brabant and of Orleance, shall make forth,
And you Prince Dolphin, with all swift dispatch
To lyne and new repayre our Townes of Warre
With men of courage, and with meanes defendant:
For England his approaches makes as fierce,
As Waters to the sucking of a Gulfe.
It fits vs then to be as prouident,
As feare may teach vs, out of late examples
Left by the fatall and neglected English,
Vpon our fields

Dolphin. My most redoubted Father,
It is most meet we arme vs 'gainst the Foe:
For Peace it selfe should not so dull a Kingdome,
(Though War nor no knowne Quarrel were in question)
But that Defences, Musters, Preparations,
Should be maintain'd, assembled, and collected,
As were a Warre in expectation.
Therefore I say, 'tis meet we all goe forth,
To view the sick and feeble parts of France:
And let vs doe it with no shew of feare,
No, with no more, then if we heard that England
Were busied with a Whitson Morris-dance:
For, my good Liege, shee is so idly King'd,
Her Scepter so phantastically borne,
By a vaine giddie shallow humorous Youth,
That feare attends her not

Const. O peace, Prince Dolphin,
You are too much mistaken in this King:
Question your Grace the late Embassadors,
With what great State he heard their Embassie,
How well supply'd with Noble Councellors,
How modest in exception; and withall,

How terrible in constant resolution:
And you shall find, his Vanities fore-spent,
Were but the out-side of the Roman Brutus,
Couering Discretion with a Coat of Folly;
As Gardeners doe with Ordure hide those Roots
That shall first spring, and be most delicate

Dolphin. Well, 'tis not so, my Lord High Constable.
But though we thinke it so, it is no matter:
In cases of defence, 'tis best to weigh
The Enemie more mightie then he seemes,
So the proportions of defence are fill'd:
Which of a weake and niggardly proiection,
Doth like a Miser spoyle his Coat, with scanting
A little Cloth

King. Thinke we King Harry strong:
And Princes, looke you strongly arme to meet him.
The Kindred of him hath beene flesht vpon vs:
And he is bred out of that bloodie straine,
That haunted vs in our familiar Pathes:
Witnesse our too much memorable shame,
When Cressy Battell fatally was strucke,
And all our Princes captiu'd, by the hand
Of that black Name, Edward, black Prince of Wales:
Whiles that his Mountaine Sire, on Mountaine standing
Vp in the Ayre, crown'd with the Golden Sunne,
Saw his Heroicall Seed, and smil'd to see him
Mangle the Worke of Nature, and deface
The Patternes, that by God and by French Fathers
Had twentie yeeres been made. This is a Stem
Of that Victorious Stock: and let vs feare
The Natiue mightinesse and fate of him.
Enter a Messenger.

Mess. Embassadors from Harry King of England,
Doe craue admittance to your Maiestie

King. Weele giue them present audience.
Goe, and bring them.
You see this Chase is hotly followed, friends

Dolphin. Turne head, and stop pursuit: for coward Dogs
Most spend their mouths, whe[n] what they seem to threaten
Runs farre before them. Good my Soueraigne
Take vp the English short, and let them know
Of what a Monarchie you are the Head:
Selfe-loue, my Liege, is not so vile a sinne,
As selfe-neglecting.
Enter Exeter.

King. From our Brother of England?
Exe. From him, and thus he greets your Maiestie:
He wills you in the Name of God Almightie,
That you deuest your selfe, and lay apart
The borrowed Glories, that by gift of Heauen,
By Law of Nature, and of Nations, longs
To him and to his Heires, namely, the Crowne,
And all wide-stretched Honors, that pertaine
By Custome, and the Ordinance of Times,
Vnto the Crowne of France: that you may know
'Tis no sinister, nor no awkward Clayme,
Pickt from the worme-holes of long-vanisht dayes,
Nor from the dust of old Obliuion rakt,
He sends you this most memorable Lyne,
In euery Branch truly demonstratiue;
Willing you ouer-looke this Pedigree:
And when you find him euenly deriu'd
From his most fam'd, of famous Ancestors,
Edward the third; he bids you then resigne
Your Crowne and Kingdome, indirectly held
From him, the Natiue and true Challenger

King. Or else what followes?

Exe. Bloody constraint: for if you hide the Crowne
Euen in your hearts, there will he rake for it.
Therefore in fierce Tempest is he comming,
In Thunder and in Earth-quake, like a Ioue:
That if requiring faile, he will compell.
And bids you, in the Bowels of the Lord,
Deliuer vp the Crowne, and to take mercie
On the poore Soules, for whom this hungry Warre
Opens his vastie Iawes: and on your head
Turning the Widdowes Teares, the Orphans Cryes,
The dead-mens Blood, the priuy Maidens Groanes,
For Husbands, Fathers, and betrothed Louers,
That shall be swallowed in this Controuersie.
This is his Clayme, his Threatning, and my Message:
Vnlesse the Dolphin be in presence here;
To whom expressely I bring greeting to

King. For vs, we will consider of this further:
To morrow shall you beare our full intent
Back to our Brother of England

Dolph. For the Dolphin,
I stand here for him: what to him from England?
Exe. Scorne and defiance, sleight regard, contempt,
And any thing that may not mis-become
The mightie Sender, doth he prize you at.
Thus sayes my King: and if your Fathers Highnesse
Doe not, in graunt of all demands at large,
Sweeten the bitter Mock you sent his Maiestie;
Hee'le call you to so hot an Answer of it,
That Caues and Wombie Vaultages of France
Shall chide your Trespas, and returne your Mock
In second Accent of his Ordinance

Dolph. Say: if my Father render faire returne,
It is against my will: for I desire
Nothing but Oddes with England.

31

To that end, as matching to his Youth and Vanitie,
I did present him with the Paris-Balls

Exe. Hee'le make your Paris Louer shake for it,
Were it the Mistresse Court of mightie Europe:
And be assur'd, you'le find a diff'rence,
As we his Subiects haue in wonder found,
Betweene the promise of his greener dayes,
And these he masters now: now he weighes Time
Euen to the vtmost Graine: that you shall reade
In your owne Losses, if he stay in France

King. To morrow shall you know our mind at full.

Flourish.

Exe. Dispatch vs with all speed, least that our King
Come here himselfe to question our delay;
For he is footed in this Land already

King. You shalbe soone dispatcht, with faire conditions.
A Night is but small breathe, and little pawse,
To answer matters of this consequence.

Exeunt.

Actus Secundus.

Flourish. Enter Chorus.

Thus with imagin'd wing our swift Scene flyes,
In motion of no lesse celeritie then that of Thought.
Suppose, that you haue seene
The well-appointed King at Douer Peer,
Embarke his Royaltie: and his braue Fleet,
With silken Streamers, the young Phebus fayning;
Play with your Fancies: and in them behold,
Vpon the Hempen Tackle, Ship-boyes climbing;
Heare the shrill Whistle, which doth order giue
To sounds confus'd: behold the threaden Sayles,
Borne with th' inuisible and creeping Wind,
Draw the huge Bottomes through the furrowed Sea,
Bresting the loftie Surge. O, doe but thinke
You stand vpon the Riuage, and behold
A Citie on th' inconstant Billowes dauncing:
For so appeares this Fleet Maiesticall,
Holding due course to Harflew. Follow, follow:
Grapple your minds to sternage of this Nauie,
And leaue your England as dead Mid-night, still,
Guarded with Grandsires, Babyes, and old Women,
Eyther past, or not arriu'd to pyth and puissance:
For who is he, whose Chin is but enricht
With one appearing Hayre, that will not follow
These cull'd and choyse-drawne Caualiers to France?
Worke, worke your Thoughts, and therein see a Siege:
Behold the Ordenance on their Carriages,
With fatall mouthes gaping on girded Harflew.
Suppose th' Embassador from the French comes back:
Tells Harry, That the King doth offer him
Katherine his Daughter, and with her to Dowrie,
Some petty and vnprofitable Dukedomes.
The offer likes not: and the nimble Gunner

With Lynstock now the diuellish Cannon touches,

Alarum, and Chambers goe off.

And downe goes all before them. Still be kind,
And eech out our performance with your mind.
Enter.

Enter the King, Exeter, Bedford, and Gloucester. Alarum: Scaling
Ladders at Harflew.

King. Once more vnto the Breach,
Deare friends, once more;
Or close the Wall vp with our English dead:
In Peace, there's nothing so becomes a man,
As modest stillnesse, and humilitie:
But when the blast of Warre blowes in our eares,
Then imitate the action of the Tyger:
Stiffen the sinewes, commune vp the blood,
Disguise faire Nature with hard-fauour'd Rage:
Then lend the Eye a terrible aspect:
Let it pry through the portage of the Head,
Like the Brasse Cannon: let the Brow o'rewhelme it,
As fearefully, as doth a galled Rocke
O're-hang and iutty his confounded Base,
Swill'd with the wild and wastfull Ocean.
Now set the Teeth, and stretch the Nosthrill wide,
Hold hard the Breath, and bend vp euery Spirit
To his full height. On, on, you Noblish English,
Whose blood is fet from Fathers of Warre-proofe:
Fathers, that like so many Alexanders,
Haue in these parts from Morne till Euen fought,
And sheath'd their Swords, for lack of argument.
Dishonour not your Mothers: now attest,
That those whom you call'd Fathers, did beget you.
Be Coppy now to men of grosser blood,
And teach them how to Warre. And you good Yeomen,

Whose Lyms were made in England; shew vs here
The mettell of your Pasture: let vs sweare,
That you are worth your breeding: which I doubt not:
For there is none of you so meane and base,
That hath not Noble luster in your eyes.
I see you stand like Grey-hounds in the slips,
Straying vpon the Start. The Game's afoot:
Follow your Spirit; and vpon this Charge,
Cry, God for Harry, England, and S[aint]. George.

Alarum, and Chambers goe off.

Enter Nim, Bardolph, Pistoll, and Boy.

Bard. On, on, on, on, on, to the breach, to the breach

Nim. 'Pray thee Corporall stay, the Knocks are too hot: and for
mine owne part, I haue not a Case of Liues: the humor of it is
too hot, that is the very plaine-Song of it

Pist. The plaine-Song is most iust: for humors doe abound:
Knocks goe and come: Gods Vassals drop and dye: and Sword and
Shield, in bloody Field, doth winne immortall fame

Boy. Would I were in a Ale-house in London, I would giue all my
fame for a Pot of Ale, and safetie

Pist. And I: If wishes would preuayle with me, my
purpose should not fayle with me; but thither would I
high

Boy. As duly, but not as truly, as Bird doth sing on
bough.
Enter Fluellen.

Flu. Vp to the breach, you Dogges; auaunt you
Cullions

Pist. Be mercifull great Duke to men of Mould: abate thy Rage,
abate thy manly Rage; abate thy Rage, great Duke. Good Bawcock
bate thy Rage: vse lenitie sweet Chuck

Nim. These be good humors: your Honor wins bad
humors.
Enter.

Boy. As young as I am, I haue obseru'd these three Swashers: I
am Boy to them all three, but all they three, though they would
serue me, could not be Man to me; for indeed three such
Antiques doe not amount to a man: for Bardolph, hee is white-
liuer'd, and red-fac'd; by the meanes whereof, a faces it out, but
fights not: for Pistoll, hee hath a killing Tongue, and a quiet
Sword; by the meanes whereof, a breakes Words, and keepes
whole Weapons: for Nim, hee hath heard, that men of few Words
are the best men, and therefore hee scornes to say his Prayers,
lest a should be thought a Coward: but his few bad Words are
matcht with as few good Deeds; for a neuer broke any mans
Head but his owne, and that was against a Post, when he was
drunke. They will steale any thing, and call it Purchase. Bardolph
stole a Lute-case, bore it twelue Leagues, and sold it for three
halfepence. Nim and Bardolph are sworne Brothers in filching:
and in Callice they stole a fire-shouell. I knew by that peece of
Seruice, the men would carry Coales. They would haue me as
familiar with mens Pockets, as their Gloues or their Hand-
kerchers: which makes much against my Manhood, if I should
take from anothers Pocket, to put into mine; for it is plaine
pocketting vp of Wrongs. I must leaue them, and seeke some
better Seruice: their Villany goes against my weake stomacke,
and therefore I must cast it vp. Enter.

Enter Gower.

Gower. Captaine Fluellen, you must come presently to the
Mynes; the Duke of Gloucester would speake with you

Flu. To the Mynes? Tell you the Duke, it is not so good to come to the Mynes: for looke you, the Mynes is not according to the disciplines of the Warre; the concauities of it is not sufficient: for looke you, th' athuersarie, you may discusse vnto the Duke, looke you, is digt himselfe foure yard vnder the Countermines: by Cheshu, I thinke a will plowe vp all, if there is not better directions

Gower. The Duke of Gloucester, to whom the Order of the Siege is giuen, is altogether directed by an Irish man, a very valiant Gentleman yfaith

Welch. It is Captaine Makmorrice, is it not?
Gower. I thinke it be

Welch. By Cheshu he is an Asse, as in the World, I will verifie as much in his Beard: he ha's no more directions in the true disciplines of the Warres, looke you, of the Roman disciplines, then is a Puppy-dog. Enter Makmorrice, and Captaine Iamy.

Gower. Here a comes, and the Scots Captaine, Captaine Iamy, with him

Welch. Captaine Iamy is a maruellous falorous Gentleman, that is certain, and of great expedition and knowledge in th' aunchiant Warres, vpon my particular knowledge of his directions: by Cheshu he will maintaine his Argument as well as any Militarie man in the World, in the disciplines of the Pristine Warres of the Romans

Scot. I say gudday, Captaine Fluellen

Welch. Godden to your Worship, good Captaine Iames

Gower. How now Captaine Mackmorrice, haue you quit the
Mynes? haue the Pioners giuen o're? Irish. By Chrish Law tish ill
done: the Worke ish giue ouer, the Trompet sound the Retreat.
By my Hand I sweare, and my fathers Soule, the Worke ish ill
done: it ish giue ouer: I would haue blowed vp the Towne, so
Chrish saue me law, in an houre. O tish ill done, tish ill done: by
my Hand tish ill done

Welch. Captaine Mackmorrice, I beseech you now, will you
voutsafe me, looke you, a few disputations with you, as partly
touching or concerning the disciplines of the Warre, the Roman
Warres, in the way of Argument, looke you, and friendly
communication: partly to satisfie my Opinion, and partly for the
satisfaction, looke you, of my Mind: as touching the direction of
the Militarie discipline, that is the Point

Scot. It sall be vary gud, gud feith, gud Captens bath, and I sall
quit you with gud leue, as I may pick occasion: that sall I mary

Irish. It is no time to discourse, so Chrish saue me: the day is hot,
and the Weather, and the Warres, and the King, and the Dukes: it
is no time to discourse, the Town is beseech'd: and the Trumpet
call vs to the breech, and we talke, and be Chrish do nothing, tis
shame for vs all: so God sa'me tis shame to stand still, it is shame
by my hand: and there is Throats to be cut, and Workes to be
done, and there ish nothing done, so Christ sa'me law

Scot. By the Mes, ere theise eyes of mine take themselues to
slomber, ayle de gud seruice, or Ile ligge i'th' grund for it; ay, or
goe to death: and Ile pay't as valorously as I may, that sal I suerly
do, that is the breff and the long: mary, I wad full faine heard
some question tween you tway

Welch. Captaine Mackmorrice, I thinke, looke you, vnder your
correction, there is not many of your Nation

Irish. Of my Nation? What ish my Nation? Ish a Villaine, and a Basterd, and a Knaue, and a Rascall. What ish my Nation? Who talkes of my Nation? Welch. Looke you, if you take the matter otherwise then is meant, Captaine Mackmorrice, peraduenture I shall thinke you doe not vse me with that affabilitie, as in discretion you ought to vse me, looke you, being as good a man as your selfe, both in the disciplines of Warre, and in the deriuation of my Birth, and in other particularities

Irish. I doe not know you so good a man as my selfe: so Chrish saue me, I will cut off your Head

Gower. Gentlemen both, you will mistake each other

Scot. A, that's a foule fault.

A Parley.

Gower. The Towne sounds a Parley

Welch. Captaine Mackmorrice, when there is more better oportunitie to be required, looke you, I will be so bold as to tell you, I know the disciplines of Warre: and there is an end. Enter.

Enter the King and all his Traine before the Gates.

King. How yet resolues the Gouernour of the Towne?
This is the latest Parle we will admit:
Therefore to our best mercy giue your selues,
Or like to men prowd of destruction,
Defie vs to our worst: for as I am a Souldier,
A Name that in my thoughts becomes me best;
If I begin the batt'rie once againe,
I will not leaue the halfe-atchieued Harflew,
Till in her ashes she lye buryed.
The Gates of Mercy shall be all shut vp,
And the flesh'd Souldier, rough and hard of heart,

In libertie of bloody hand, shall raunge
With Conscience wide as Hell, mowing like Grasse
Your fresh faire Virgins, and your flowring Infants.
What is it then to me, if impious Warre,
Arrayed in flames like to the Prince of Fiends,
Doe with his smyrcht complexion all fell feats,
Enlynckt to wast and desolation?
What is't to me, when you your selues are cause,
If your pure Maydens fall into the hand
Of hot and forcing Violation?
What Reyne can hold licentious Wickednesse,
When downe the Hill he holds his fierce Carriere?
We may as bootlesse spend our vaine Command
Vpon th' enraged Souldiers in their spoyle,
As send Precepts to the Leuiathan, to come ashore.
Therefore, you men of Harflew,
Take pitty of your Towne and of your People,
Whiles yet my Souldiers are in my Command,
Whiles yet the coole and temperate Wind of Grace
O're-blowes the filthy and contagious Clouds
Of heady Murther, Spoyle, and Villany.
If not: why in a moment looke to see
The blind and bloody Souldier, with foule hand
Desire the Locks of your shrill-shriking Daughters:
Your Fathers taken by the siluer Beards,
And their most reuerend Heads dasht to the Walls:
Your naked Infants spitted vpon Pykes,
Whiles the mad Mothers, with their howles confus'd,
Doe breake the Clouds; as did the Wiues of Iewry,
At Herods bloody-hunting slaughter-men.
What say you? Will you yeeld, and this auoyd?
Or guiltie in defence, be thus destroy'd.
Enter Gouernour.

Gouer. Our expectation hath this day an end:
The Dolphin, whom of Succours we entreated,
Returnes vs, that his Powers are yet not ready,

To rayse so great a Siege: Therefore great King,
We yeeld our Towne and Liues to thy soft Mercy:
Enter our Gates, dispose of vs and ours,
For we no longer are defensible

King. Open your Gates: Come Vnckle Exeter,
Goe you and enter Harflew; there remaine,
And fortifie it strongly 'gainst the French:
Vse mercy to them all for vs, deare Vnckle.
The Winter comming on, and Sicknesse growing
Vpon our Souldiers, we will retyre to Calis.
To night in Harflew will we be your Guest,
To morrow for the March are we addrest.

Flourish, and enter the Towne.

Enter Katherine and an old Gentlewoman.

Kathe. Alice, tu as este en Angleterre, & tu bien parlas le
Language

Alice. En peu Madame

Kath. Ie te prie m' ensigniez, il faut que ie apprend a parlen:
Comient appelle vous le main en Anglois?
Alice. Le main il & appelle de Hand

Kath. De Hand

Alice. E le doyts

Kat. Le doyts, ma foy Ie oublie, e doyt mays, ie me souemeray
le doyts ie pense qu'ils ont appelle de fingres, ou de fingres

Alice. Le main de Hand, le doyts le Fingres, ie pense que ie
suis le bon escholier

Kath. I'ay gaynie diux mots d' Anglois vistement, coment appelle vous le ongles?
Alice. Le ongles, les appellons de Nayles

Kath. De Nayles escoute: dites moy, si ie parle bien: de Hand, de Fingres, e de Nayles

Alice. C'est bien dict Madame, il & fort bon Anglois

Kath. Dites moy l' Anglois pour le bras

Alice. De Arme, Madame

Kath. E de coudee

Alice. D' Elbow

Kath. D' Elbow: Ie men fay le repiticio de touts les mots que vous maves, apprins des a present

Alice. Il & trop difficile Madame, comme Ie pense

Kath. Excuse moy Alice escoute, d' Hand, de Fingre, de Nayles, d' Arma, de Bilbow

Alice. D' Elbow, Madame

Kath. O Seigneur Dieu, ie men oublie d' Elbow, coment appelle vous le col

Alice. De Nick, Madame

Kath. De Nick, e le menton

Alice. De Chin

Kath. De Sin: le col de Nick, le menton de Sin

Alice. Ouy. Sauf vostre honneur en verite vous pronouncies les mots ausi droict, que le Natifs d' Angleterre

Kath. Ie ne doute point d' apprendre par de grace de Dieu, & en peu de temps

Alice. N' aue vos y desia oublie ce que ie vous a ensignie

Kath. Nome ie recitera a vous promptement, d' Hand, de Fingre, de Maylees

Alice. De Nayles, Madame

Kath. De Nayles, de Arme, de Ilbow

Alice. Sans vostre honeus d' Elbow

Kath. Ainsi de ie d' Elbow, de Nick, & de Sin: coment appelle vous les pied & de roba

Alice. Le Foot Madame, & le Count

Kath. Le Foot, & le Count: O Seignieur Dieu, il sont le mots de son mauvais corruptible grosse & impudique, & non pour le Dames de Honeur d' vser: Ie ne voudray pronouncer ce mots deuant le Seigneurs de France, pour toute le monde, fo le Foot & le Count, neant moys, Ie recitera vn autrefoys ma lecon ensembe, d' Hand, de Fingre, de Nayles, d' Arme, d' Elbow, de Nick, de Sin, de Foot, le Count

Alice. Excellent, Madame

Kath. C'est asses pour vne foyes, alons nous a diner.
Enter.

Enter the King of France, the Dolphin, the Constable of France,
and others.

King. 'Tis certaine he hath past the Riuer Some

Const. And if he be not fought withall, my Lord,
Let vs not liue in France: let vs quit all,
And giue our Vineyards to a barbarous People

Dolph. O Dieu viuant: Shall a few Sprayes of vs,
The emptying of our Fathers Luxurie,
Our Syens, put in wilde and sauage Stock,
Spirt vp so suddenly into the Clouds,
And ouer-looke their Grafters?
Brit. Normans, but bastard Normans, Norman bastards:
Mort du ma vie, if they march along
Vnfought withall, but I will sell my Dukedome,
To buy a slobbry and a durtie Farme
In that nooke-shotten Ile of Albion

Const. Dieu de Battailes, where haue they this mettell?
Is not their Clymate foggy, raw, and dull?
On whom, as in despight, the Sunne lookes pale,
Killing their Fruit with frownes. Can sodden Water,
A Drench for sur-reyn'd Iades, their Barly broth,
Decoct their cold blood to such valiant heat?
And shall our quick blood, spirited with Wine,
Seeme frostie? O, for honor of our Land,
Let vs not hang like roping Isyckles
Vpon our Houses Thatch, whiles a more frostie People
Sweat drops of gallant Youth in our rich fields:
Poore we call them, in their Natiue Lords

Dolphin. By Faith and Honor,
Our Madames mock at vs, and plainely say,
Our Mettell is bred out, and they will giue
Their bodyes to the Lust of English Youth,

To new-store France with Bastard Warriors

Brit. They bid vs to the English Dancing-Schooles,
And teach Lauolta's high, and swift Carranto's,
Saying, our Grace is onely in our Heeles,
And that we are most loftie Run-awayes

King. Where is Montioy the Herald? speed him hence,
Let him greet England with our sharpe defiance.
Vp Princes, and with spirit of Honor edged,
More sharper then your Swords, high to the field:
Charles Delabreth, High Constable of France,
You Dukes of Orleance, Burbon, and of Berry,
Alanson, Brabant, Bar, and Burgonie,
Iaques Chattillion, Rambures, Vandemont,
Beumont, Grand Pree, Roussi, and Faulconbridge,
Loys, Lestrale, Bouciquall, and Charaloyes,
High Dukes, great Princes, Barons, Lords, and Kings;
For your great Seats, now quit you of great shames:
Barre Harry England, that sweepes through our Land
With Penons painted in the blood of Harflew:
Rush on his Hoast, as doth the melted Snow
Vpon the Valleyes, whose low Vassall Seat,
The Alpes doth spit, and void his rhewme vpon.
Goe downe vpon him, you haue Power enough,
And in a Captiue Chariot, into Roan
Bring him our Prisoner

Const. This becomes the Great.
Sorry am I his numbers are so few,
His Souldiers sick, and famisht in their March:
For I am sure, when he shall see our Army,
Hee'le drop his heart into the sinck of feare,
And for atchieuement, offer vs his Ransome

King. Therefore Lord Constable, hast on Montioy,
And let him say to England, that we send,

To know what willing Ransome he will giue.
Prince Dolphin, you shall stay with vs in Roan

Dolph. Not so, I doe beseech your Maiestie

King. Be patient, for you shall remaine with vs.
Now forth Lord Constable, and Princes all,
And quickly bring vs word of Englands fall.

Exeunt.

Enter Captaines, English and Welch, Gower and Fluellen.

Gower. How now Captaine Fluellen, come you from
the Bridge?
Flu. I assure you, there is very excellent Seruices committed
at the Bridge

Gower. Is the Duke of Exeter safe? Flu. The Duke of Exeter is as
magnanimous as Agamemnon, and a man that I loue and honour
with my soule, and my heart, and my dutie, and my liue, and my
liuing, and my vttermost power. He is not, God be praysed and
blessed, any hurt in the World, but keepes the Bridge most
valiantly, with excellent discipline. There is an aunchient
Lieutenant there at the Pridge, I thinke in my very conscience
hee is as valiant a man as Marke Anthony, and hee is a man of no
estimation in the World, but I did see him doe as gallant seruice

Gower. What doe you call him?
Flu. Hee is call'd aunchient Pistoll

Gower. I know him not.
Enter Pistoll.

Flu. Here is the man

Pist. Captaine, I thee beseech to doe me fauours: the

Duke of Exeter doth loue thee well

Flu. I, I prayse God, and I haue merited some loue at
his hands

Pist. Bardolph, a Souldier firme and sound of heart, and of
buxome valour, hath by cruell Fate, and giddie Fortunes furious
fickle Wheele, that Goddesse blind, that stands vpon the rolling
restlesse Stone

Flu. By your patience, aunchient Pistoll: Fortune is painted blinde,
with a Muffler afore his eyes, to signifie to you, that Fortune is
blinde; and shee is painted also with a Wheele, to signifie to you,
which is the Morall of it, that shee is turning and inconstant, and
mutabilitie, and variation: and her foot, looke you, is fixed vpon a
Sphericall Stone, which rowles, and rowles, and rowles: in good
truth, the Poet makes a most excellent description of it: Fortune
is an excellent Morall

Pist. Fortune is Bardolphs foe, and frownes on him: for he hath
stolne a Pax, and hanged must a be: a damned death: let
Gallowes gape for Dogge, let Man goe free, and let not Hempe his
Wind-pipe suffocate: but Exeter hath giuen the doome of death,
for Pax of little price. Therefore goe speake, the Duke will heare
thy voyce; and let not Bardolphs vitall thred bee cut with edge of
Penny-Cord, and vile reproach. Speake Captaine for his Life, and I
will thee requite

Flu. Aunchient Pistoll, I doe partly vnderstand your meaning

Pist. Why then reioyce therefore

Flu. Certainly Aunchient, it is not a thing to reioyce at: for if,
looke you, he were my Brother, I would desire the Duke to vse
his good pleasure, and put him to execution; for discipline ought
to be vsed

Pist. Dye, and be dam'd, and Figo for thy friendship

Flu. It is well

Pist. The Figge of Spaine.
Enter.

Flu. Very good

Gower. Why, this is an arrant counterfeit Rascall, I remember him now: a Bawd, a Cut-purse

Flu. Ile assure you, a vtt'red as praue words at the Pridge, as you shall see in a Summers day: but it is very well: what he ha's spoke to me, that is well I warrant you, when time is serue

Gower. Why 'tis a Gull, a Foole, a Rogue, that now and then goes to the Warres, to grace himselfe at his returne into London, vnder the forme of a Souldier: and such fellowes are perfit in the Great Commanders Names, and they will learne you by rote where Seruices were done; at such and such a Sconce, at such a Breach, at such a Conuoy: who came off brauely, who was shot, who disgrac'd, what termes the Enemy stood on: and this they conne perfitly in the phrase of Warre; which they tricke vp with new-tuned Oathes: and what a Beard of the Generalls Cut, and a horride Sute of the Campe, will doe among foming Bottles, and Ale-washt Wits, is wonderfull to be thought on: but you must learne to know such slanders of the age, or else you may be maruellously mistooke

Flu. I tell you what, Captaine Gower: I doe perceiue hee is not the man that hee would gladly make shew to the World hee is: if I finde a hole in his Coat, I will tell him my minde: hearke you, the King is comming, and I must speake with him from the Pridge.

Drum and Colours. Enter the King and his poore Souldiers.

Flu. God plesse your Maiestie

King. How now Fluellen, cam'st thou from the Bridge? Flu. I, so please your Maiestie: The Duke of Exeter ha's very gallantly maintain'd the Pridge; the French is gone off, looke you, and there is gallant and most praue passages: marry, th' athuersarie was haue possession of the Pridge, but he is enforced to retyre, and the Duke of Exeter is Master of the Pridge: I can tell your Maiestie, the Duke is a praue man

King. What men haue you lost, Fluellen? Flu. The perdition of th' athuersarie hath beene very great, reasonnable great: marry for my part, I thinke the Duke hath lost neuer a man, but one that is like to be executed for robbing a Church, one Bardolph, if your Maiestie know the man: his face is all bubukles and whelkes, and knobs, and flames a fire, and his lippes blowes at his nose, and it is like a coale of fire, sometimes plew, and sometimes red, but his nose is executed, and his fire's out

King. Wee would haue all such offendors so cut off: and we giue expresse charge, that in our Marches through the Countrey, there be nothing compell'd from the Villages; nothing taken, but pay'd for: none of the French vpbrayded or abused in disdainefull Language; for when Leuitie and Crueltie play for a Kingdome, the gentler Gamester is the soonest winner.

Tucket. Enter Mountioy.

Mountioy. You know me by my habit

King. Well then, I know thee: what shall I know of thee?
Mountioy. My Masters mind

King. Vnfold it

49

Mountioy. Thus sayes my King: Say thou to Harry of England,
Though we seem'd dead, we did but sleepe: Aduantage is a better
Souldier then rashnesse. Tell him, wee could haue rebuk'd him at
Harflewe, but that wee thought not good to bruise an iniurie, till
it were full ripe. Now wee speake vpon our Q. and our voyce is
imperiall: England shall repent his folly, see his weakenesse, and
admire our sufferance. Bid him therefore consider of his
ransome, which must proportion the losses we haue borne, the
subiects we haue lost, the disgrace we haue digested; which in
weight to re-answer, his pettinesse would bow vnder. For our
losses, his Exchequer is too poore; for th' effusion of our bloud,
the Muster of his Kingdome too faint a number; and for our
disgrace, his owne person kneeling at our feet, but a weake and
worthlesse satisfaction. To this adde defiance: and tell him for
conclusion, he hath betrayed his followers, whose condemnation
is pronounc't: So farre my King and Master; so much my Office

King. What is thy name? I know thy qualitie

Mount. Mountioy

King. Thou doo'st thy Office fairely. Turne thee backe,
And tell thy King, I doe not seeke him now,
But could be willing to march on to Callice,
Without impeachment: for to say the sooth,
Though 'tis no wisdome to confesse so much
Vnto an enemie of Craft and Vantage,
My people are with sicknesse much enfeebled,
My numbers lessen'd: and those few I haue,
Almost no better then so many French;
Who when they were in health, I tell thee Herald,
I thought, vpon one payre of English Legges
Did march three Frenchmen. Yet forgiue me God,
That I doe bragge thus; this your ayre of France
Hath blowne that vice in me. I must repent:
Goe therefore tell thy Master, heere I am;
My Ransome, is this frayle and worthlesse Trunke;

My Army, but a weake and sickly Guard:
Yet God before, tell him we will come on,
Though France himselfe, and such another Neighbor
Stand in our way. There's for thy labour Mountioy.
Goe bid thy Master well aduise himselfe.
If we may passe, we will: if we be hindred,
We shall your tawnie ground with your red blood
Discolour: and so Mountioy, fare you well.
The summe of all our Answer is but this:
We would not seeke a Battaile as we are,
Nor as we are, we say we will not shun it:
So tell your Master

Mount. I shall deliuer so: Thankes to your Highnesse

Glouc. I hope they will not come vpon vs now

King. We are in Gods hand, Brother, not in theirs:
March to the Bridge, it now drawes toward night,
Beyond the Riuer wee'le encampe our selues,
And on to morrow bid them march away.

Exeunt.

Enter the Constable of France, the Lord Ramburs, Orleance,
Dolphin, with others.

Const. Tut, I haue the best Armour of the World:
would it were day

Orleance. You haue an excellent Armour: but let my
Horse haue his due

Const. It is the best Horse of Europe

Orleance. Will it neuer be Morning?
Dolph. My Lord of Orleance, and my Lord High Constable,

you talke of Horse and Armour?
Orleance. You are as well prouided of both, as any
Prince in the World

Dolph. What a long Night is this? I will not change my Horse
with any that treades but on foure postures: ch' ha: he bounds
from the Earth, as if his entrayles were hayres: le Cheual volante,
the Pegasus, ches les narines de feu. When I bestryde him, I
soare, I am a Hawke: he trots the ayre: the Earth sings, when he
touches it: the basest horne of his hoofe, is more Musicall then
the Pipe of Hermes

Orleance. Hee's of the colour of the Nutmeg

Dolph. And of the heat of the Ginger. It is a Beast for Perseus: hee
is pure Ayre and Fire; and the dull Elements of Earth and Water
neuer appeare in him, but only in patient stillnesse while his
Rider mounts him: hee is indeede a Horse, and all other lades
you may call Beasts

Const. Indeed my Lord, it is a most absolute and excellent
Horse

Dolph. It is the Prince of Palfrayes, his Neigh is like the bidding of
a Monarch, and his countenance enforces Homage

Orleance. No more Cousin

Dolph. Nay, the man hath no wit, that cannot from the rising of
the Larke to the lodging of the Lambe, varie deserued prayse on
my Palfray: it is a Theame as fluent as the Sea: Turne the Sands
into eloquent tongues, and my Horse is argument for them all:
'tis a subiect for a Soueraigne to reason on, and for a Soueraignes
Soueraigne to ride on: And for the World, familiar to vs, and
vnknowne, to lay apart their particular Functions, and wonder at
him, I once writ a Sonnet in his prayse, and began thus, Wonder
of Nature

Orleance. I haue heard a Sonnet begin so to ones Mistresse

Dolph. Then did they imitate that which I compos'd to my
Courser, for my Horse is my Mistresse

Orleance. Your Mistresse beares well

Dolph. Me well, which is the prescript prayse and perfection
of a good and particular Mistresse

Const. Nay, for me thought yesterday your Mistresse
shrewdly shooke your back

Dolph. So perhaps did yours

Const. Mine was not bridled

Dolph. O then belike she was old and gentle, and you rode like a
Kerne of Ireland, your French Hose off, and in your strait
Strossers

Const. You haue good iudgement in Horsemanship

Dolph. Be warn'd by me then: they that ride so, and ride not
warily, fall into foule Boggs: I had rather haue my Horse to my
Mistresse

Const. I had as liue haue my Mistresse a Iade

Dolph. I tell thee Constable, my Mistresse weares his
owne hayre

Const. I could make as true a boast as that, if I had a
Sow to my Mistresse

Dolph. Le chien est retourne a son propre vemissement est

la leuye lauee au bourbier: thou mak'st vse of any thing

Const. Yet doe I not vse my Horse for my Mistresse,
or any such Prouerbe, so little kin to the purpose

Ramb. My Lord Constable, the Armour that I saw in
your Tent to night, are those Starres or Sunnes vpon it?
Const. Starres my Lord

Dolph. Some of them will fall to morrow, I hope

Const. And yet my Sky shall not want

Dolph. That may be, for you beare a many superfluously,
and 'twere more honor some were away

Const. Eu'n as your Horse beares your prayses, who
would trot as well, were some of your bragges dismounted

Dolph. Would I were able to loade him with his desert. Will it
neuer be day? I will trot to morrow a mile, and my way shall be
paued with English Faces

Const. I will not say so, for feare I should be fac't out of my way:
but I would it were morning, for I would faine be about the
eares of the English

Ramb. Who will goe to Hazard with me for twentie
Prisoners?
Const. You must first goe your selfe to hazard, ere you
haue them

Dolph. 'Tis Mid-night, Ile goe arme my selfe.
Enter.

Orleance. The Dolphin longs for morning

Ramb. He longs to eate the English

Const. I thinke he will eate all he kills

Orleance. By the white Hand of my Lady, hee's a gallant
Prince

Const. Sweare by her Foot, that she may tread out the
Oath

Orleance. He is simply the most actiue Gentleman of
France

Const. Doing is actiuitie, and he will still be doing

Orleance. He neuer did harme, that I heard of

Const. Nor will doe none to morrow: hee will keepe that good
name still

Orleance. I know him to be valiant

Const. I was told that, by one that knowes him better
then you

Orleance. What's hee?
Const. Marry hee told me so himselfe, and hee sayd hee
car'd not who knew it

Orleance. Hee needes not, it is no hidden vertue in
him

Const. By my faith Sir, but it is: neuer any body saw it, but his
Lacquey: 'tis a hooded valour, and when it appeares, it will bate

Orleance. Ill will neuer sayd well

Const. I will cap that Prouerbe with, There is flatterie
in friendship

Orleance. And I will take vp that with, Giue the Deuill
his due

Const. Well plac't: there stands your friend for the
Deuill: haue at the very eye of that Prouerbe with, A
Pox of the Deuill

Orleance. You are the better at Prouerbs, by how much
a Fooles Bolt is soone shot

Const. You haue shot ouer

Orleance. 'Tis not the first time you were ouer-shot.
Enter a Messenger.

Mess. My Lord high Constable, the English lye within
fifteene hundred paces of your Tents

Const. Who hath measur'd the ground?
Mess. The Lord Grandpree

Const. A valiant and most expert Gentleman. Would it were day?
Alas poore Harry of England: hee longs not for the Dawning, as
wee doe

Orleance. What a wretched and peeuish fellow is this King of
England, to mope with his fat-brain'd followers so farre out of his
knowledge

Const. If the English had any apprehension, they
would runne away

Orleance. That they lack: for if their heads had any intellectuall
Armour, they could neuer weare such heauie

56

Head-pieces

Ramb. That Iland of England breedes very valiant
Creatures; their Mastiffes are of vnmatchable courage

Orleance. Foolish Curres, that runne winking into the mouth of a
Russian Beare, and haue their heads crusht like rotten Apples:
you may as well say, that's a valiant Flea, that dare eate his
breakefast on the Lippe of a Lyon

Const. Iust, iust: and the men doe sympathize with the Mastiffes,
in robustious and rough comming on, leauing their Wits with
their Wiues: and then giue them great Meales of Beefe, and Iron
and Steele; they will eate like Wolues, and fight like Deuils

Orleance. I, but these English are shrowdly out of
Beefe

Const. Then shall we finde to morrow, they haue only stomackes
to eate, and none to fight. Now is it time to arme: come, shall we
about it? Orleance. It is now two a Clock: but let me see, by ten
Wee shall haue each a hundred English men.

Exeunt.

HENRY V

Actus Tertius.

Chorus.

Now entertaine coniecture of a time,
When creeping Murmure and the poring Darke
Fills the wide Vessell of the Vniuerse.
From Camp to Camp, through the foule Womb of Night
The Humme of eyther Army stilly sounds;
That the fixt Centinels almost receiue
The secret Whispers of each others Watch.
Fire answers fire, and through their paly flames
Each Battaile sees the others vmber'd face.
Steed threatens Steed, in high and boastfull Neighs
Piercing the Nights dull Eare: and from the Tents,
The Armourers accomplishing the Knights,
With busie Hammers closing Riuets vp,
Giue dreadfull note of preparation.
The Countrey Cocks doe crow, the Clocks doe towle:
And the third howre of drowsie Morning nam'd,
Prowd of their Numbers, and secure in Soule,
The confident and ouer-lustie French,
Doe the low-rated English play at Dice;
And chide the creeple-tardy-gated Night,
Who like a foule and ougly Witch doth limpe
So tediously away. The poore condemned English,
Like Sacrifices, by their watchfull Fires
Sit patiently, and inly ruminate
The Mornings danger: and their gesture sad,
Inuesting lanke-leane Cheekes, and Warre-worne Coats,
Presented them vnto the gazing Moone
So many horride Ghosts. O now, who will behold
The Royall Captaine of this ruin'd Band
Walking from Watch to Watch, from Tent to Tent;
Let him cry, Prayse and Glory on his head:
For forth he goes, and visits all his Hoast,

Bids them good morrow with a modest Smyle,
And calls them Brothers, Friends, and Countreymen.
Vpon his Royall Face there is no note,
How dread an Army hath enrounded him;
Nor doth he dedicate one iot of Colour
Vnto the wearie and all-watched Night:
But freshly lookes, and ouer-beares Attaint,
With chearefull semblance, and sweet Maiestie:
That euery Wretch, pining and pale before,
Beholding him, plucks comfort from his Lookes.
A Largesse vniuersall, like the Sunne,
His liberall Eye doth giue to euery one,
Thawing cold feare, that meane and gentle all
Behold, as may vnworthinesse define.
A little touch of Harry in the Night,
And so our Scene must to the Battaile flye:
Where, O for pitty, we shall much disgrace,
With foure or fiue most vile and ragged foyles,
(Right ill dispos'd, in brawle ridiculous)
The Name of Agincourt: Yet sit and see,
Minding true things, by what their Mock'ries bee.
Enter.

Enter the King, Bedford, and Gloucester.

King. Gloster, 'tis true that we are in great danger,
The greater therefore should our Courage be.
God morrow Brother Bedford: God Almightie,
There is some soule of goodnesse in things euill,
Would men obseruingly distill it out.
For our bad Neighbour makes vs early stirrers,
Which is both healthfull, and good husbandry.
Besides, they are our outward Consciences,
And Preachers to vs all; admonishing,
That we should dresse vs fairely for our end.
Thus may we gather Honey from the Weed,
And make a Morall of the Diuell himselfe.

Enter Erpingham.

Good morrow old Sir Thomas Erpingham:
A good soft Pillow for that good white Head,
Were better then a churlish turfe of France

Erping. Not so my Liege, this Lodging likes me better,
Since I may say, now lye I like a King

King. 'Tis good for men to loue their present paines,
Vpon example, so the Spirit is eased:
And when the Mind is quickned, out of doubt
The Organs, though defunct and dead before,
Breake vp their drowsie Graue, and newly moue
With casted slough, and fresh legeritie.
Lend me thy Cloake Sir Thomas: Brothers both,
Commend me to the Princes in our Campe;
Doe my good morrow to them, and anon
Desire them all to my Pauillion

Gloster. We shall, my Liege

Erping. Shall I attend your Grace?
King. No, my good Knight:
Goe with my Brothers to my Lords of England:
I and my Bosome must debate a while,
And then I would no other company

Erping. The Lord in Heauen blesse thee, Noble
Harry.

Exeunt.

King. God a mercy old Heart, thou speak'st chearefully.
Enter Pistoll

Pist. Che vous la?

King. A friend

Pist. Discusse vnto me, art thou Officer, or art thou
base, common, and popular?
King. I am a Gentleman of a Company

Pist. Trayl'st thou the puissant Pyke?
King. Euen so: what are you?
Pist. As good a Gentleman as the Emperor

King. Then you are a better then the King

Pist. The King's a Bawcock, and a Heart of Gold, a
Lad of Life, an Impe of Fame, of Parents good, of Fist
most valiant: I kisse his durtie shooe, and from heartstring
I loue the louely Bully. What is thy Name?
King. Harry le Roy

Pist. Le Roy? a Cornish Name: art thou of Cornish Crew?
King. No, I am a Welchman

Pist. Know'st thou Fluellen?
King. Yes

Pist. Tell him Ile knock his Leeke about his Pate vpon
S[aint]. Dauies day

King. Doe not you weare your Dagger in your Cappe
that day, least he knock that about yours

Pist. Art thou his friend?
King. And his Kinsman too

Pist. The Figo for thee then

King. I thanke you: God be with you

Pist. My name is Pistol call'd.
Enter.

King. It sorts well with your fiercenesse.

Manet King.

Enter Fluellen and Gower.

Gower. Captaine Fluellen

Flu. 'So, in the Name of Iesu Christ, speake fewer: it is the
greatest admiration in the vniuersall World, when the true and
aunchient Prerogatifes and Lawes of the Warres is not kept: if
you would take the paines but to examine the Warres of Pompey
the Great, you shall finde, I warrant you, that there is no tiddle
tadle nor pibble bable in Pompeyes Campe: I warrant you, you
shall finde the Ceremonies of the Warres, and the Cares of it, and
the Formes of it, and the Sobrietie of it, and the Modestie of it, to
be otherwise

Gower. Why the Enemie is lowd, you heare him all
Night

Flu. If the Enemie is an Asse and a Foole, and a prating
Coxcombe; is it meet, thinke you, that wee should also, looke
you, be an Asse and a Foole, and a prating Coxcombe, in your
owne conscience now? Gow. I will speake lower

Flu. I pray you, and beseech you, that you will.
Enter.

King. Though it appeare a little out of fashion,
There is much care and valour in this Welchman.
Enter three Souldiers, Iohn Bates, Alexander Court, and Michael
Williams.

Court. Brother Iohn Bates, is not that the Morning
which breakes yonder?
Bates. I thinke it be: but wee haue no great cause to
desire the approach of day

Williams. Wee see yonder the beginning of the day,
but I thinke wee shall neuer see the end of it. Who goes
there?
King. A Friend

Williams. Vnder what Captaine serue you?
King. Vnder Sir Iohn Erpingham

Williams. A good old Commander, and a most kinde
Gentleman: I pray you, what thinkes he of our estate?
King. Euen as men wrackt vpon a Sand, that looke to
be washt off the next Tyde

Bates. He hath not told his thought to the King? King. No: nor it
is not meet he should: for though I speake it to you, I thinke the
King is but a man, as I am: the Violet smells to him, as it doth to
me; the Element shewes to him, as it doth to me; all his Sences
haue but humane Conditions: his Ceremonies layd by, in his
Nakednesse he appeares but a man; and though his affections are
higher mounted then ours, yet when they stoupe, they stoupe
with the like wing: therefore, when he sees reason of feares, as
we doe; his feares, out of doubt, be of the same rellish as ours
are: yet in reason, no man should possesse him with any
appearance of feare; least hee, by shewing it, should dis-hearten
his Army

Bates. He may shew what outward courage he will: but I
beleeue, as cold a Night as 'tis, hee could wish himselfe in
Thames vp to the Neck; and so I would he were, and I by him, at
all aduentures, so we were quit here

King. By my troth, I will speake my conscience of the King: I
thinke hee would not wish himselfe any where, but where hee is

Bates. Then I would he were here alone; so should he be sure to
be ransomed, and a many poore mens liues saued

King. I dare say, you loue him not so ill, to wish him here alone:
howsoeuer you speake this to feele other mens minds, me thinks
I could not dye any where so contented, as in the Kings
company; his Cause being iust, and his Quarrell honorable

Williams. That's more then we know

Bates. I, or more then wee should seeke after; for wee know
enough, if wee know wee are the Kings Subiects: if his Cause be
wrong, our obedience to the King wipes the Cryme of it out of vs

Williams. But if the Cause be not good, the King himselfe hath a
heauie Reckoning to make, when all those Legges, and Armes,
and Heads, chopt off in a Battaile, shall ioyne together at the
latter day, and cry all, Wee dyed at such a place, some swearing,
some crying for a Surgean; some vpon their Wiues, left poore
behind them; some vpon the Debts they owe, some vpon their
Children rawly left: I am afear'd, there are few dye well, that dye
in a Battaile: for how can they charitably dispose of any thing,
when Blood is their argument? Now, if these men doe not dye
well, it will be a black matter for the King, that led them to it;
who to disobey, were against all proportion of subiection

King. So, if a Sonne that is by his Father sent about Merchandize,
doe sinfully miscarry vpon the Sea; the imputation of his
wickednesse, by your rule, should be imposed vpon his Father
that sent him: or if a Seruant, vnder his Masters command,
transporting a summe of Money, be assayled by Robbers, and dye
in many irreconcil'd Iniquities; you may call the businesse of the
Master the author of the Seruants damnation: but this is not so:
The King is not bound to answer the particular endings of his

Souldiers, the Father of his Sonne, nor the Master of his Seruant;
for they purpose not their death, when they purpose their
seruices. Besides, there is no King, be his Cause neuer so
spotlesse, if it come to the arbitrement of Swords, can trye it out
with all vnspotted Souldiers: some (peraduenture) haue on them
the guilt of premeditated and contriued Murther; some, of
beguiling Virgins with the broken Seales of Periurie; some,
making the Warres their Bulwarke, that haue before gored the
gentle Bosome of Peace with Pillage and Robberie. Now, if these
men haue defeated the Law, and outrunne Natiue punishment;
though they can out-strip men, they haue no wings to flye from
God. Warre is his Beadle, Warre is his Vengeance: so that here
men are punisht, for before breach of the Kings Lawes, in now
the Kings Quarrell: where they feared the death, they haue borne
life away; and where they would bee safe, they perish. Then if
they dye vnprouided, no more is the King guiltie of their
damnation, then hee was before guiltie of those Impieties, for
the which they are now visited. Euery Subiects Dutie is the Kings,
but euery Subiects Soule is his owne. Therefore should euery
Souldier in the Warres doe as euery sicke man in his Bed, wash
euery Moth out of his Conscience: and dying so, Death is to him
aduantage; or not dying, the time was blessedly lost, wherein
such preparation was gayned: and in him that escapes, it were
not sinne to thinke, that making God so free an offer, he let him
outliue that day, to see his Greatnesse, and to teach others how
they should prepare

Will. 'Tis certaine, euery man that dyes ill, the ill vpon
his owne head, the King is not to answer it

Bates. I doe not desire hee should answer for me, and
yet I determine to fight lustily for him

King. I my selfe heard the King say he would not be
ransom'd

Will. I, hee said so, to make vs fight chearefully: but when our
throats are cut, hee may be ransom'd, and wee ne're the wiser

King. If I liue to see it, I will neuer trust his word after

Will. You pay him then: that's a perillous shot out of an Elder
Gunne, that a poore and a priuate displeasure can doe against a
Monarch: you may as well goe about to turne the Sunne to yce,
with fanning in his face with a Peacocks feather: You'le neuer
trust his word after; come, 'tis a foolish saying

King. Your reproofe is something too round, I should
be angry with you, if the time were conuenient

Will. Let it bee a Quarrell betweene vs, if you
liue

King. I embrace it

Will. How shall I know thee againe?
King. Giue me any Gage of thine, and I will weare it
in my Bonnet: Then if euer thou dar'st acknowledge it,
I will make it my Quarrell

Will. Heere's my Gloue: Giue mee another of
thine

King. There

Will. This will I also weare in my Cap: if euer thou come to me,
and say, after to morrow, This is my Gloue, by this Hand I will
take thee a box on the eare

King. If euer I liue to see it, I will challenge it

Will. Thou dar'st as well be hang'd

King. Well, I will doe it, though I take thee in the
Kings companie

Will. Keepe thy word: fare thee well

Bates. Be friends you English fooles, be friends, wee haue French
Quarrels enow, if you could tell how to reckon.

Exit Souldiers.

King. Indeede the French may lay twentie French
Crownes to one, they will beat vs, for they beare them
on their shoulders: but it is no English Treason to cut
French Crownes, and to morrow the King himselfe will
be a Clipper.
Vpon the King, let vs our Liues, our Soules,
Our Debts, our carefull Wiues,
Our Children, and our Sinnes, lay on the King:
We must beare all.
O hard Condition, Twin-borne with Greatnesse,
Subiect to the breath of euery foole, whose sence
No more can feele, but his owne wringing.
What infinite hearts-ease must Kings neglect,
That priuate men enioy?
And what haue Kings, that Priuates haue not too,
Saue Ceremonie, saue generall Ceremonie?
And what art thou, thou Idoll Ceremonie?
What kind of God art thou? that suffer'st more
Of mortall griefes, then doe thy worshippers.
What are thy Rents? what are thy Commings in?
O Ceremonie, shew me but thy worth.
What? is thy Soule of Odoration?
Art thou ought else but Place, Degree, and Forme,
Creating awe and feare in other men?
Wherein thou art lesse happy, being fear'd,
Then they in fearing.
What drink'st thou oft, in stead of Homage sweet,

But poyson'd flatterie? O, be sick, great Greatnesse,
And bid thy Ceremonie giue thee cure.
Thinks thou the fierie Feuer will goe out
With Titles blowne from Adulation?
Will it giue place to flexure and low bending?
Canst thou, when thou command'st the beggers knee,
Command the health of it? No, thou prowd Dreame,
That play'st so subtilly with a Kings Repose.
I am a King that find thee: and I know,
'Tis not the Balme, the Scepter, and the Ball,
The Sword, the Mase, the Crowne Imperiall,
The enter-tissued Robe of Gold and Pearle,
The farsed Title running 'fore the King,
The Throne he sits on: nor the Tyde of Pompe,
That beates vpon the high shore of this World:
No, not all these, thrice-gorgeous Ceremonie;
Not all these, lay'd in Bed Maiesticall,
Can sleepe so soundly, as the wretched Slaue:
Who with a body fill'd, and vacant mind,
Gets him to rest, cram'd with distressefull bread,
Neuer sees horride Night, the Child of Hell:
But like a Lacquey, from the Rise to Set,
Sweates in the eye of Phebus; and all Night
Sleepes in Elizium: next day after dawne,
Doth rise and helpe Hiperio[n] to his Horse,
And followes so the euer-running yeere
With profitable labour to his Graue:
And but for Ceremonie, such a Wretch,
Winding vp Dayes with toyle, and Nights with sleepe,
Had the fore-hand and vantage of a King.
The Slaue, a Member of the Countreyes peace,
Enioyes it; but in grosse braine little wots,
What watch the King keepes, to maintaine the peace;
Whose howres, the Pesant best aduantages.
Enter Erpingham.

Erp. My Lord, your Nobles iealous of your absence,

Seeke through your Campe to find you

King. Good old Knight, collect them all together
At my Tent: Ile be before thee

Erp. I shall doo't, my Lord.
Enter.

King. O God of Battailes, steele my Souldiers hearts,
Possesse them not with feare: Take from them now
The sence of reckning of th' opposed numbers:
Pluck their hearts from them. Not to day, O Lord,
O not to day, thinke not vpon the fault
My Father made, in compassing the Crowne.
I Richards body haue interred new,
And on it haue bestowed more contrite teares,
Then from it issued forced drops of blood.
Fiue hundred poore I haue in yeerely pay,
Who twice a day their wither'd hands hold vp
Toward Heauen, to pardon blood:
And I haue built two Chauntries,
Where the sad and solemne Priests sing still
For Richards Soule. More will I doe:
Though all that I can doe, is nothing worth;
Since that my Penitence comes after all,
Imploring pardon.
Enter Gloucester.

Glouc. My Liege

King. My Brother Gloucesters voyce? I:
I know thy errand, I will goe with thee:
The day, my friend, and all things stay for me.

Exeunt.

Enter the Dolphin, Orleance, Ramburs, and Beaumont.

Orleance. The Sunne doth gild our Armour vp, my
Lords

Dolph. Monte Cheual: My Horse, Verlot Lacquay:
Ha

Orleance. Oh braue Spirit

Dolph. Via les ewes & terre

Orleance. Rien puis le air & feu

Dolph. Cein, Cousin Orleance.
Enter Constable.

Now my Lord Constable? Const. Hearke how our Steedes, for
present Seruice neigh

Dolph. Mount them, and make incision in their Hides,
That their hot blood may spin in English eyes,
And doubt them with superfluous courage: ha

Ram. What, wil you haue them weep our Horses blood?
How shall we then behold their naturall teares?
Enter Messenger.

Messeng. The English are embattail'd, you French
Peeres

Const. To Horse you gallant Princes, straight to Horse.
Doe but behold yond poore and starued Band,
And your faire shew shall suck away their Soules,
Leauing them but the shales and huskes of men.
There is not worke enough for all our hands,
Scarce blood enough in all their sickly Veines,
To giue each naked Curtleax a stayne,

That our French Gallants shall to day draw out,
And sheath for lack of sport. Let vs but blow on them,
The vapour of our Valour will o're-turne them.
'Tis positiue against all exceptions, Lords,
That our superfluous Lacquies, and our Pesants,
Who in vnnecessarie action swarme
About our Squares of Battaile, were enow
To purge this field of such a hilding Foe;
Though we vpon this Mountaines Basis by,
Tooke stand for idle speculation:
But that our Honours must not. What's to say?
A very little little let vs doe,
And all is done: then let the Trumpets sound
The Tucket Sonuance, and the Note to mount:
For our approach shall so much dare the field,
That England shall couch downe in feare, and yeeld.
Enter Graundpree.

Grandpree. Why do you stay so long, my Lords of France?
Yond Iland Carrions, desperate of their bones,
Ill-fauoredly become the Morning field:
Their ragged Curtaines poorely are let loose,
And our Ayre shakes them passing scornefully.
Bigge Mars seemes banqu'rout in their begger'd Hoast,
And faintly through a rustie Beuer peepes.
The Horsemen sit like fixed Candlesticks,
With Torch-staues in their hand: and their poore Iades
Lob downe their heads, dropping the hides and hips:
The gumme downe roping from their pale-dead eyes,
And in their pale dull mouthes the Iymold Bitt
Lyes foule with chaw'd-grasse, still and motionlesse.
And their executors, the knauish Crowes,
Flye o're them all, impatient for their howre.
Description cannot sute it selfe in words,
To demonstrate the Life of such a Battaile,
In life so liuelesse, as it shewes it selfe

Const. They haue said their prayers,
And they stay for death

Dolph. Shall we goe send them Dinners, and fresh Sutes,
And giue their fasting Horses Prouender,
And after fight with them?
Const. I stay but for my Guard: on
To the field, I will the Banner from a Trumpet take,
And vse it for my haste. Come, come away,
The Sunne is high, and we out-weare the day.

Exeunt.

Enter Gloucester, Bedford, Exeter, Erpingham with all his Hoast:
Salisbury, and Westmerland.

Glouc. Where is the King?
Bedf. The King himselfe is rode to view their Battaile

West. Of fighting men they haue full threescore thousand

Exe. There's fiue to one, besides they all are fresh

Salisb. Gods Arme strike with vs, 'tis a fearefull oddes.
God buy' you Princes all; Ile to my Charge:
If we no more meet, till we meet in Heauen;
Then ioyfully, my Noble Lord of Bedford,
My deare Lord Gloucester, and my good Lord Exeter,
And my kind Kinsman, Warriors all, adieu

Bedf. Farwell good Salisbury, & good luck go with thee:
And yet I doe thee wrong, to mind thee of it,
For thou art fram'd of the firme truth of valour

Exe. Farwell kind Lord: fight valiantly to day

Bedf. He is as full of Valour as of Kindnesse,

73

Princely in both.
Enter the King.

West. O that we now had here
But one ten thousand of those men in England,
That doe no worke to day

King. What's he that wishes so?
My Cousin Westmerland. No, my faire Cousin:
If we are markt to dye, we are enow
To doe our Countrey losse: and if to liue,
The fewer men, the greater share of honour.
Gods will, I pray thee wish not one man more.
By Ioue, I am not couetous for Gold,
Nor care I who doth feed vpon my cost:
It yernes me not, if men my Garments weare;
Such outward things dwell not in my desires.
But if it be a sinne to couet Honor,
I am the most offending Soule aliue.
No 'faith, my Couze, wish not a man from England:
Gods peace, I would not loose so great an Honor,
As one man more me thinkes would share from me,
For the best hope I haue. O, doe not wish one more:
Rather proclaime it (Westmerland) through my Hoast,
That he which hath no stomack to this fight,
Let him depart, his Pasport shall be made,
And Crownes for Conuoy put into his Purse:
We would not dye in that mans companie,
That feares his fellowship, to dye with vs.
This day is call'd the Feast of Crispian:
He that out-liues this day, and comes safe home,
Will stand a tip-toe when this day is named,
And rowse him at the Name of Crispian.
He that shall see this day, and liue old age,
Will yeerely on the Vigil feast his neighbours,
And say, to morrow is Saint Crispian.
Then will he strip his sleeue, and shew his skarres:

Old men forget; yet all shall be forgot:
But hee'le remember, with aduantages,
What feats he did that day. Then shall our Names,
Familiar in his mouth as household words,
Harry the King, Bedford and Exeter,
Warwick and Talbot, Salisbury and Gloucester,
Be in their flowing Cups freshly remembred.
This story shall the good man teach his sonne:
And Crispine Crispian shall ne're goe by,
From this day to the ending of the World,
But we in it shall be remembred;
We few, we happy few, we band of brothers:
For he to day that sheds his blood with me,
Shall be my brother: be he ne're so vile,
This day shall gentle his Condition.
And Gentlemen in England, now a bed,
Shall thinke themselues accurst they were not here;
And hold their Manhoods cheape, whiles any speakes,
That fought with vs vpon Saint Crispines day.
Enter Salisbury.

Sal. My Soueraign Lord, bestow your selfe with speed:
The French are brauely in their battailes set,
And will with all expedience charge on vs

King. All things are ready, if our minds be so

West. Perish the man, whose mind is backward now

King. Thou do'st not wish more helpe from England,
Couze?
West. Gods will, my Liege, would you and I alone,
Without more helpe, could fight this Royall battaile

King. Why now thou hast vnwisht fiue thousand men:
Which likes me better, then to wish vs one.
You know your places: God be with you all.

Tucket. Enter Montioy.

Mont. Once more I come to know of thee King Harry,
If for thy Ransome thou wilt now compound,
Before thy most assured Ouerthrow:
For certainly, thou art so neere the Gulfe,
Thou needs must be englutted. Besides, in mercy
The Constable desires thee, thou wilt mind
Thy followers of Repentance; that their Soules
May make a peacefull and a sweet retyre
From off these fields: where (wretches) their poore bodies
Must lye and fester

King. Who hath sent thee now?
Mont. The Constable of France

King. I pray thee beare my former Answer back:
Bid them atchieue me, and then sell my bones.
Good God, why should they mock poore fellowes thus?
The man that once did sell the Lyons skin
While the beast liu'd, was kill'd with hunting him.
A many of our bodyes shall no doubt
Find Natiue Graues: vpon the which, I trust
Shall witnesse liue in Brasse of this dayes worke.
And those that leaue their valiant bones in France,
Dying like men, though buryed in your Dunghills,
They shall be fam'd: for there the Sun shall greet them,
And draw their honors reeking vp to Heauen,
Leauing their earthly parts to choake your Clyme,
The smell whereof shall breed a Plague in France.
Marke then abounding valour in our English:
That being dead, like to the bullets crasing,
Breake out into a second course of mischiefe,
Killing in relapse of Mortalitie.
Let me speake prowdly: Tell the Constable,
We are but Warriors for the working day:

Our Gaynesse and our Gilt are all besmyrcht
With raynie Marching in the painefull field.
There's not a piece of feather in our Hoast:
Good argument (I hope) we will not flye:
And time hath worne vs into slouenrie.
But by the Masse, our hearts are in the trim:
And my poore Souldiers tell me, yet ere Night,
They'le be in fresher Robes, or they will pluck
The gay new Coats o're the French Souldiers heads,
And turne them out of seruice. If they doe this,
As if God please, they shall; my Ransome then
Will soone be leuyed.
Herauld, saue thou thy labour:
Come thou no more for Ransome, gentle Herauld,
They shall haue none, I sweare, but these my ioynts:
Which if they haue, as I will leaue vm them,
Shall yeeld them little, tell the Constable

Mont. I shall, King Harry. And so fare thee well:
Thou neuer shalt heare Herauld any more.
Enter.

King. I feare thou wilt once more come againe for a
Ransome.
Enter Yorke.

Yorke. My Lord, most humbly on my knee I begge
The leading of the Vaward

King. Take it, braue Yorke.
Now Souldiers march away,
And how thou pleasest God, dispose the day.

Exeunt.

Alarum. Excursions. Enter Pistoll, French Souldier, Boy.

77

Pist. Yeeld Curre

French. Ie pense que vous estes le Gentilhome de bon qualitee

Pist. Qualtitie calmie custure me. Art thou a Gentleman?
What is thy Name? discusse

French. O Seigneur Dieu

Pist. O Signieur Dewe should be a Gentleman: perpend my words
O Signieur Dewe, and marke: O Signieur Dewe, thou dyest on
point of Fox, except O Signieur thou doe giue to me egregious
Ransome

French. O prennes miserecordie aye pitez de moy

Pist. Moy shall not serue, I will haue fortie Moyes: for
I will fetch thy rymme out at thy Throat, in droppes of
Crimson blood

French. Est il impossible d' eschapper le force de ton bras

Pist. Brasse, Curre? thou damned and luxurious Mountaine
Goat, offer'st me Brasse?
French. O perdonne moy

Pist. Say'st thou me so? is that a Tonne of Moyes?
Come hither boy, aske me this slaue in French what is his
Name

Boy. Escoute comment estes vous appelle?
French. Mounsieur le Fer

Boy. He sayes his Name is M. Fer

Pist. M. Fer: Ile fer him, and firke him, and ferret him:
discusse the same in French vnto him

Boy. I doe not know the French for fer, and ferret, and
firke

Pist. Bid him prepare, for I will cut his throat

French. Que dit il Mounsieur?
Boy. Il me commande a vous dire que vous faite vous
prest, car ce soldat icy est disposee tout asture de couppes vostre
gorge

Pist. Owy, cuppele gorge permafoy pesant, vnlesse thou giue me
Crownes, braue Crownes; or mangled shalt thou be by this my
Sword

French. O Ie vous supplie pour l' amour de Dieu: ma pardonner,
Ie suis le Gentilhome de bon maison, garde ma vie, & Ie vous
donneray deux cent escus

Pist. What are his words?
Boy. He prayes you to saue his life, he is a Gentleman
of a good house, and for his ransom he will giue you two
hundred Crownes

Pist. Tell him my fury shall abate, and I the Crownes
will take

Fren. Petit Monsieur que dit il?
Boy. Encore qu'il et contra son Iurement, de pardonner aucune
prisonner: neantmons pour les escues que vous layt a promets,
il est content a vous donnes le liberte le franchisement

Fre. Sur mes genoux se vous donnes milles remercious, et
Ie me estime heurex que Ie intombe, entre les main d' vn
Cheualier
Ie pense le plus braue valiant et tres distime signieur
d' Angleterre

Pist. Expound vnto me boy

Boy. He giues you vpon his knees a thousand thanks, and he esteemes himselfe happy, that he hath falne into the hands of one (as he thinkes) the most braue, valorous and thrice-worthy signeur of England

Pist. As I sucke blood, I will some mercy shew. Follow mee

Boy. Saaue vous le grand Capitaine? I did neuer know so full a voyce issue from so emptie a heart: but the saying is true, The empty vessel makes the greatest sound, Bardolfe and Nym had tenne times more valour, then this roaring diuell i'th olde play, that euerie one may payre his nayles with a woodden dagger, and they are both hang'd, and so would this be, if hee durst steale any thing aduenturously. I must stay with the Lackies with the luggage of our camp, the French might haue a good pray of vs, if he knew of it, for there is none to guard it but boyes. Enter.

Enter Constable, Orleance, Burbon, Dolphin, and Rambures.

Con. O Diable

Orl. O signeur le iour et perdia, toute et perdie

Dol. Mor Dieu ma vie, all is confounded all,
Reproach, and euerlasting shame
Sits mocking in our Plumes.

A short Alarum.

O meschante Fortune, do not runne away

Con. Why all our rankes are broke

Dol. O perdurable shame, let's stab our selues:

Be these the wretches that we plaid at dice for?
Orl. Is this the King we sent too, for his ransome?
Bur. Shame, and eternall shame, nothing but shame,
Let vs dye in once more backe againe,
And he that will not follow Burbon now,
Let him go hence, and with his cap in hand
Like a base Pander hold the Chamber doore,
Whilst a base slaue, no gentler then my dogge,
His fairest daughter is contaminated

Con. Disorder that hath spoyl'd vs, friend vs now,
Let vs on heapes go offer vp our liues

Orl. We are enow yet liuing in the Field,
To smother vp the English in our throngs,
If any order might be thought vpon

Bur. The diuell take Order now, Ile to the throng;
Let life be short, else shame will be too long.
Enter.

Alarum. Enter the King and his trayne, with Prisoners.

King. Well haue we done, thrice-valiant Countrimen,
But all's not done, yet keepe the French the field

Exe. The D[uke]. of York commends him to your Maiesty
King. Liues he good Vnckle: thrice within this houre
I saw him downe; thrice vp againe, and fighting,
From Helmet to the spurre, all blood he was

Exe. In which array (braue Soldier) doth he lye,
Larding the plaine: and by his bloody side,
(Yoake-fellow to his honour-owing-wounds)
The Noble Earle of Suffolke also lyes.
Suffolke first dyed, and Yorke all hagled ouer
Comes to him, where in gore he lay insteeped,

And takes him by the Beard, kisses the gashes
That bloodily did yawne vpon his face.
He cryes aloud; Tarry my Cosin Suffolke,
My soule shall thine keepe company to heauen:
Tarry (sweet soule) for mine, then flye a-brest:
As in this glorious and well-foughten field
We kept together in our Chiualrie.
Vpon these words I came, and cheer'd him vp,
He smil'd me in the face, raught me his hand,
And with a feeble gripe, sayes: Deere my Lord,
Commend my seruice to my Soueraigne,
So did he turne, and ouer Suffolkes necke
He threw his wounded arme, and kist his lippes,
And so espous'd to death, with blood he seal'd
A Testament of Noble-ending-loue:
The prettie and sweet manner of it forc'd
Those waters from me, which I would haue stop'd,
But I had not so much of man in mee,
And all my mother came into mine eyes,
And gaue me vp to teares

King. I blame you not,
For hearing this, I must perforce compound
With mixtfull eyes, or they will issue to.

Alarum

But hearke, what new alarum is this same?
The French haue re-enforc'd their scatter'd men:
Then euery souldiour kill his Prisoners,
Giue the word through.

Exit

Actus Quartus.

Enter Fluellen and Gower.

Flu. Kill the poyes and the luggage, 'Tis expressely against the
Law of Armes, tis as arrant a peece of knauery marke you now,
as can bee offert in your Conscience now, is it not? Gow. Tis
certaine, there's not a boy left aliue, and the Cowardly Rascalls
that ranne from the battaile ha' done this slaughter: besides they
haue burned and carried away all that was in the Kings Tent,
wherefore the King most worthily hath caus'd euery soldiour to
cut his prisoners throat. O 'tis a gallant King

Flu. I, hee was porne at Monmouth Captaine Gower:
What call you the Townes name where Alexander the
pig was borne?
Gow. Alexander the Great

Flu. Why I pray you, is not pig, great? The pig, or the great, or the
mighty, or the huge, or the magnanimous, are all one reckonings,
saue the phrase is a litle variations

Gower. I thinke Alexander the Great was borne in Macedon, his
Father was called Phillip of Macedon, as I take it

Flu. I thinke it is in Macedon where Alexander is porne: I tell you
Captaine, if you looke in the Maps of the Orld, I warrant you sall
finde in the comparisons betweene Macedon & Monmouth, that
the situations looke you, is both alike. There is a Riuer in
Macedon, & there is also moreouer a Riuer at Monmouth, it is
call'd Wye at Monmouth: but it is out of my praines, what is the
name of the other Riuer: but 'tis all one, tis alike as my fingers is
to my fingers, and there is Salmons in both. If you marke
Alexanders life well, Harry of Monmouthes life is come after it
indifferent well, for there is figures in all things. Alexander God
knowes, and you know, in his rages, and his furies, and his

wraths, and his chollers, and his moodes, and his displeasures, and his indignations, and also being a little intoxicates in his praines, did in his Ales and his angers (looke you) kill his best friend Clytus

Gow. Our King is not like him in that, he neuer kill'd any of his friends

Flu. It is not well done (marke you now) to take the tales out of my mouth, ere it is made and finished. I speak but in the figures, and comparisons of it: as Alexander kild his friend Clytus, being in his Ales and his Cuppes; so also Harry Monmouth being in his right wittes, and his good iudgements, turn'd away the fat Knight with the great belly doublet: he was full of iests, and gypes, and knaueries, and mockes, I haue forgot his name

Gow. Sir Iohn Falstaffe

Flu. That is he: Ile tell you, there is good men porne at Monmouth

Gow. Heere comes his Maiesty.

Alarum. Enter King Harry and Burbon with prisoners. Flourish.

King. I was not angry since I came to France,
Vntill this instant. Take a Trumpet Herald,
Ride thou vnto the Horsemen on yond hill:
If they will fight with vs, bid them come downe,
Or voyde the field: they do offend our sight.
If they'l do neither, we will come to them,
And make them sker away, as swift as stones
Enforced from the old Assyrian slings:
Besides, wee'l cut the throats of those we haue,
And not a man of them that we shall take,
Shall taste our mercy. Go and tell them so.
Enter Montioy.

Exe. Here comes the Herald of the French, my Liege
Glou. His eyes are humbler then they vs'd to be

King. How now, what meanes this Herald? Knowst
thou not,
That I haue fin'd these bones of mine for ransome?
Com'st thou againe for ransome?
Her. No great King:
I come to thee for charitable License,
That we may wander ore this bloody field,
To booke our dead, and then to bury them,
To sort our Nobles from our common men.
For many of our Princes (woe the while)
Lye drown'd and soak'd in mercenary blood:
So do our vulgar drench their peasant limbes
In blood of Princes, and with wounded steeds
Fret fet-locke deepe in gore, and with wilde rage
Yerke out their armed heeles at their dead masters,
Killing them twice. O giue vs leaue great King,
To view the field in safety, and dispose
Of their dead bodies

Kin. I tell thee truly Herald,
I know not if the day be ours or no,
For yet a many of your horsemen peere,
And gallop ore the field

Her. The day is yours

Kin. Praised be God, and not our strength for it:
What is this Castle call'd that stands hard by

Her. They call it Agincourt

King. Then call we this the field of Agincourt,
Fought on the day of Crispin Crispianus

Flu. Your Grandfather of famous memory (an't please your
Maiesty) and your great Vncle Edward the Placke Prince of Wales,
as I haue read in the Chronicles, fought a most praue pattle here
in France

Kin. They did Fluellen

Flu. Your Maiesty sayes very true: If your Maiesties is remembred
of it, the Welchmen did good seruice in a Garden where Leekes
did grow, wearing Leekes in their Monmouth caps, which your
Maiesty know to this houre is an honourable badge of the
seruice: And I do beleeue your Maiesty takes no scorne to weare
the Leeke vppon S[aint]. Tauies day

King. I weare it for a memorable honor:
For I am Welch you know good Countriman

Flu. All the water in Wye, cannot wash your Maiesties
Welsh plood out of your pody, I can tell you that:
God plesse it, and preserue it, as long as it pleases his
Grace, and his Maiesty too

Kin. Thankes good my Countrymen

Flu. By Ieshu, I am your Maiesties Countreyman, I care not who
know it: I will confesse it to all the Orld, I need not to be
ashamed of your Maiesty, praised be God so long as your Maiesty
is an honest man

King. Good keepe me so.
Enter Williams.

Our Heralds go with him,
Bring me iust notice of the numbers dead
On both our parts. Call yonder fellow hither

Exe. Souldier, you must come to the King

Kin. Souldier, why wear'st thou that Gloue in thy
Cappe?
Will. And't please your Maiesty, tis the gage of one
that I should fight withall, if he be aliue

Kin. An Englishman? Wil. And't please your Maiesty, a Rascall that
swagger'd with me last night: who if aliue, and euer dare to
challenge this Gloue, I haue sworne to take him a boxe a'th ere:
or if I can see my Gloue in his cappe, which he swore as he was a
Souldier he would weare (if aliue) I wil strike it out soundly

Kin. What thinke you Captaine Fluellen, is it fit this
souldier keepe his oath

Flu. Hee is a Crauen and a Villaine else, and't please
your Maiesty in my conscience

King. It may bee, his enemy is a Gentleman of great
sort quite from the answer of his degree

Flu. Though he be as good a lentleman as the diuel is, as Lucifer
and Belzebub himselfe, it is necessary (looke your Grace) that he
keepe his vow and his oath: If hee bee periur'd (see you now) his
reputation is as arrant a villaine and a Iacke sawce, as euer his
blacke shoo trodd vpon Gods ground, and his earth, in my
conscience law King. Then keepe thy vow sirrah, when thou
meet'st the fellow

Wil. So, I wil my Liege, as I liue

King. Who seru'st thou vnder?
Will. Vnder Captaine Gower, my Liege

Flu. Gower is a good Captaine, and is good knowledge
and literatured in the Warres

King. Call him hither to me, Souldier

Will. I will my Liege.
Enter.

King. Here Fluellen, weare thou this fauour for me, and sticke it
in thy Cappe: when Alanson and my selfe were downe together, I
pluckt this Gloue from his Helme: If any man challenge this, hee
is a friend to Alanson, and an enemy to our Person; if thou
encounter any such, apprehend him, and thou do'st me loue

Flu. Your Grace doo's me as great Honors as can be desir'd in the
hearts of his Subiects: I would faine see the man, that ha's but
two legges, that shall find himselfe agreefd at this Gloue; that is
all: but I would faine see it once, and please God of his grace that
I might see

King. Know'st thou Gower?
Flu. He is my deare friend, and please you

King. Pray thee goe seeke him, and bring him to my
Tent

Flu. I will fetch him.
Enter.

King. My Lord of Warwick, and my Brother Gloster,
Follow Fluellen closely at the heeles.
The Gloue which I haue giuen him for a fauour,
May haply purchase him a box a'th' eare.
It is the Souldiers: I by bargaine should
Weare it my selfe. Follow good Cousin Warwick:
If that the Souldier strike him, as I iudge
By his blunt bearing, he will keepe his word;
Some sodaine mischiefe may arise of it:
For I doe know Fluellen valiant,

And toucht with Choler, hot as Gunpowder,
And quickly will returne an iniurie.
Follow, and see there be no harme betweene them.
Goe you with me, Vnckle of Exeter.

Exeunt.

Enter Gower and Williams.

Will. I warrant it is to Knight you, Captaine.
Enter Fluellen.

Flu. Gods will, and his pleasure, Captaine, I beseech you now,
come apace to the King: there is more good toward you
peraduenture, then is in your knowledge to dreame of

Will. Sir, know you this Gloue?
Flu. Know the Gloue? I know the Gloue is a Gloue

Will. I know this, and thus I challenge it.

Strikes him.

Flu. 'Sblud, an arrant Traytor as anyes in the Vniuersall
World, or in France, or in England

Gower. How now Sir? you Villaine

Will. Doe you thinke Ile be forsworne?
Flu. Stand away Captaine Gower, I will giue Treason
his payment into plowes, I warrant you

Will. I am no Traytor

Flu. That's a Lye in thy Throat. I charge you in his
Maiesties Name apprehend him, he's a friend of the Duke
Alansons.

Enter Warwick and Gloucester.

Warw. How now, how now, what's the matter? Flu. My Lord of
Warwick, heere is, praysed be God for it, a most contagious
Treason come to light, looke you, as you shall desire in a
Summers day. Heere is his Maiestie. Enter King and Exeter.

King. How now, what's the matter?
Flu. My Liege, heere is a Villaine, and a Traytor,
that looke your Grace, ha's strooke the Gloue which
your Maiestie is take out of the Helmet of Alanson

Will. My Liege, this was my Gloue, here is the fellow of it: and he
that I gaue it to in change, promis'd to weare it in his Cappe: I
promis'd to strike him, if he did: I met this man with my Gloue
in his Cappe, and I haue been as good as my word

Flu. Your Maiestie heare now, sauing your Maiesties Manhood,
what an arrant rascally, beggerly, lowsie Knaue it is: I hope your
Maiestie is peare me testimonie and witnesse, and will
auouchment, that this is the Gloue of Alanson, that your Maiestie
is giue me, in your Conscience now

King. Giue me thy Gloue Souldier;
Looke, heere is the fellow of it:
'Twas I indeed thou promised'st to strike,
And thou hast giuen me most bitter termes

Flu. And please your Maiestie, let his Neck answere
for it, if there is any Marshall Law in the World

King. How canst thou make me satisfaction?
Will. All offences, my Lord, come from the heart: neuer
came any from mine, that might offend your Maiestie

King. It was our selfe thou didst abuse

Will. Your Maiestie came not like your selfe: you appear'd to me
but as a common man; witnesse the Night, your Garments, your
Lowlinesse: and what your Highnesse suffer'd vnder that shape, I
beseech you take it for your owne fault, and not mine: for had
you beene as I tooke you for, I made no offence; therefore I
beseech your Highnesse pardon me

King. Here Vnckle Exeter, fill this Gloue with Crownes,
And giue it to this fellow. Keepe it fellow,
And weare it for an Honor in thy Cappe,
Till I doe challenge it. Giue him the Crownes:
And Captaine, you must needs be friends with him

Flu. By this Day and this Light, the fellow ha's mettell enough in
his belly: Hold, there is twelue-pence for you, and I pray you to
serue God, and keepe you out of prawles and prabbles, and
quarrels and dissentions, and I warrant you it is the better for
you

Will. I will none of your Money

Flu. It is with a good will: I can tell you it will serue you to mend
your shooes: come, wherefore should you be so pashfull, your
shooes is not so good: 'tis a good silling I warrant you, or I will
change it. Enter Herauld.

King. Now Herauld, are the dead numbred?
Herald. Heere is the number of the slaught'red
French

King. What Prisoners of good sort are taken,
Vnckle?
Exe. Charles Duke of Orleance, Nephew to the King,
Iohn Duke of Burbon, and Lord Bouchiquald:
Of other Lords and Barons, Knights and Squires,
Full fifteene hundred, besides common men

King. This Note doth tell me of ten thousand French
That in the field lye slaine: of Princes in this number,
And Nobles bearing Banners, there lye dead
One hundred twentie six: added to these,
Of Knights, Esquires, and gallant Gentlemen,
Eight thousand and foure hundred: of the which,
Fiue hundred were but yesterday dubb'd Knights.
So that in these ten thousand they haue lost,
There are but sixteene hundred Mercenaries:
The rest are Princes, Barons, Lords, Knights, Squires,
And Gentlemen of bloud and qualitie.
The Names of those their Nobles that lye dead:
Charles Delabreth, High Constable of France,
Iaques of Chatilion, Admirall of France,
The Master of the Crosse-bowes, Lord Rambures,
Great Master of France, the braue Sir Guichard Dolphin,
Iohn Duke of Alanson, Anthonie Duke of Brabant,
The Brother to the Duke of Burgundie,
And Edward Duke of Barr: of lustie Earles,
Grandpree and Roussie, Fauconbridge and Foyes,
Beaumont and Marle, Vandemont and Lestrale.
Here was a Royall fellowship of death.
Where is the number of our English dead?
Edward the Duke of Yorke, the Earle of Suffolke,
Sir Richard Ketly, Dauy Gam Esquire;
None else of name: and of all other men,
But fiue and twentie.
O God, thy Arme was heere:
And not to vs, but to thy Arme alone,
Ascribe we all: when, without stratagem,
But in plaine shock, and euen play of Battaile,
Was euer knowne so great and little losse?
On one part and on th' other, take it God,
For it is none but thine

Exet. 'Tis wonderfull

King. Come, goe we in procession to the Village:
And be it death proclaymed through our Hoast,
To boast of this, or take that prayse from God,
Which is his onely

Flu. Is it not lawfull and please your Maiestie, to tell
how many is kill'd?
King. Yes Captaine: but with this acknowledgement,
That God fought for vs

Flu. Yes, my conscience, he did vs great good

King. Doe we all holy Rights:
Let there be sung Non nobis, and Te Deum,
The dead with charitie enclos'd in Clay:
And then to Callice, and to England then,
Where ne're from France arriu'd more happy men.

Exeunt.

HENRY V

Actus Quintus.

Enter Chorus.

Vouchsafe to those that haue not read the Story,
That I may prompt them: and of such as haue,
I humbly pray them to admit th' excuse
Of time, of numbers, and due course of things,
Which cannot in their huge and proper life,
Be here presented. Now we beare the King
Toward Callice: Graunt him there; there seene,
Heaue him away vpon your winged thoughts,
Athwart the Sea: Behold the English beach
Pales in the flood; with Men, Wiues, and Boyes,
Whose shouts & claps out-voyce the deep-mouth'd Sea,
Which like a mightie Whiffler 'fore the King,
Seemes to prepare his way: So let him land,
And solemnly see him set on to London.
So swift a pace hath Thought, that euen now
You may imagine him vpon Black-Heath:
Where, that his Lords desire him, to haue borne
His bruised Helmet, and his bended Sword
Before him, through the Citie: he forbids it,
Being free from vainnesse, and selfe-glorious pride;
Giuing full Trophee, Signall, and Ostent,
Quite from himselfe, to God. But now behold,
In the quick Forge and working-house of Thought,
How London doth powre out her Citizens,
The Maior and all his Brethren in best sort,
Like to the Senatours of th' antique Rome,
With the Plebeians swarming at their heeles,
Goe forth and fetch their Conqu'ring Cæsar in:
As by a lower, but by louing likelyhood,
Were now the Generall of our gracious Empresse,
As in good time he may, from Ireland comming,
Bringing Rebellion broached on his Sword;

How many would the peacefull Citie quit,
To welcome him? much more, and much more cause,
Did they this Harry. Now in London place him.
As yet the lamentation of the French
Inuites the King of Englands stay at home:
The Emperour's comming in behalfe of France,
To order peace betweene them: and omit
All the occurrences, what euer chanc't,
Till Harryes backe returne againe to France:
There must we bring him; and my selfe haue play'd
The interim, by remembring you 'tis past.
Then brooke abridgement, and your eyes aduance,
After your thoughts, straight backe againe to France.
Enter.

Enter Fluellen and Gower.

Gower. Nay, that's right: but why weare you your
Leeke to day? S[aint]. Dauies day is past

Flu. There is occasions and causes why and wherefore in all
things: I will tell you asse my friend, Captaine Gower; the
rascally, scauld, beggerly, lowsie, pragging Knaue Pistoll, which
you and your selfe, and all the World, know to be no petter then
a fellow, looke you now, of no merits: hee is come to me, and
prings me pread and sault yesterday, looke you, and bid me eate
my Leeke: it was in a place where I could not breed no
contention with him; but I will be so bold as to weare it in my
Cap till I see him once againe, and then I will tell him a little
piece of my desires. Enter Pistoll.

Gower. Why heere hee comes, swelling like a Turkycock

Flu. 'Tis no matter for his swellings, nor his Turkycocks.
God plesse you aunchient Pistoll: you scuruie lowsie
Knaue, God plesse you

Pist. Ha, art thou bedlam? doest thou thirst, base
Troian, to haue me fold vp Parcas fatall Web? Hence;
I am qualmish at the smell of Leeke

Flu. I peseech you heartily, scuruie lowsie Knaue, at my desires,
and my requests, and my petitions, to eate, looke you, this Leeke;
because, looke you, you doe not loue it, nor your affections, and
your appetites and your disgestions doo's not agree with it, I
would desire you to eate it

Pist. Not for Cadwallader and all his Goats

Flu. There is one Goat for you.

Strikes him.

Will you be so good, scauld Knaue, as eate it?
Pist. Base Troian, thou shalt dye

Flu. You say very true, scauld Knaue, when Gods will is: I will
desire you to liue in the meane time, and eate your Victuals:
come, there is sawce for it. You call'd me yesterday Mountaine-
Squier, but I will make you to day a squire of low degree. I pray
you fall too, if you can mocke a Leeke, you can eate a Leeke

Gour. Enough Captaine, you haue astonisht him

Flu. I say, I will make him eate some part of my leeke, or I will
peate his pate foure dayes: bite I pray you, it is good for your
greene wound, and your ploodie Coxecombe

Pist. Must I bite

Flu. Yes certainly, and out of doubt and out of question
too, and ambiguities

Pist. By this Leeke, I will most horribly reuenge I

eate and eate I sweare

Flu. Eate I pray you, will you haue some more sauce
to your Leeke: there is not enough Leeke to sweare by

Pist. Quiet thy Cudgell, thou dost see I eate

Flu. Much good do you scald knaue, heartily. Nay, pray you
throw none away, the skinne is good for your broken Coxcombe;
when you take occasions to see Leekes heereafter, I pray you
mocke at 'em, that is all

Pist. Good

Flu. I, Leekes is good: hold you, there is a groat to
heale your pate

Pist. Me a groat?
Flu. Yes verily, and in truth you shall take it, or I haue
another Leeke in my pocket, which you shall eate

Pist. I take thy groat in earnest of reuenge

Flu. If I owe you any thing, I will pay you in Cudgels, you shall be
a Woodmonger, and buy nothing of me but cudgels: God bu'y
you, and keepe you, & heale your pate.

Exit

Pist. All hell shall stirre for this

Gow. Go, go, you are a counterfeit cowardly Knaue, will you
mocke at an ancient Tradition began vppon an honourable
respect, and worne as a memorable Trophee of predeceased
valor, and dare not auouch in your deeds any of your words. I
haue seene you gleeking & galling at this Gentleman twice or
thrice. You thought, because he could not speake English in the

natiue garb, he could not therefore handle an English Cudgell:
you finde it otherwise, and henceforth let a Welsh correction,
teach you a good English condition, fare ye well.

Exit

Pist. Doeth fortune play the huswife with me now?
Newes haue I that my Doll is dead i'th Spittle of a malady
of France, and there my rendeuous is quite cut off:
Old I do waxe, and from my wearie limbes honour is
Cudgeld. Well, Baud Ile turne, and something leane to
Cut-purse of quicke hand: To England will I steale, and
there Ile steale:
And patches will I get vnto these cudgeld scarres,
And swore I got them in the Gallia warres.
Enter.

Enter at one doore, King Henry, Exeter, Bedford, Warwicke, and
other
Lords. At another, Queene Isabel, the King, the Duke of
Bourgougne, and
other French.

King. Peace to this meeting, wherefore we are met;
Vnto our brother France, and to our Sister
Health and faire time of day: Ioy and good wishes
To our most faire and Princely Cosine Katherine:
And as a branch and member of this Royalty,
By whom this great assembly is contriu'd,
We do salute you Duke of Burgogne,
And Princes French and Peeres health to you all

Fra. Right ioyous are we to behold your face,
Most worthy brother England, fairely met,
So are you Princes (English) euery one

Quee. So happy be the Issue brother Ireland

Of this good day, and of this gracious meeting,
As we are now glad to behold your eyes,
Your eyes which hitherto haue borne
In them against the French that met them in their bent,
The fatall Balls of murthering Basiliskes:
The venome of such Lookes we fairely hope
Haue lost their qualitie, and that this day
Shall change all griefes and quarrels into loue

Eng. To cry Amen to that, thus we appeare

Quee. You English Princes all, I doe salute you

Burg. My dutie to you both, on equall loue.
Great Kings of France and England: that I haue labour'd
With all my wits, my paines, and strong endeuors,
To bring your most Imperiall Maiesties
Vnto this Barre, and Royall enterview;
Your Mightinesse on both parts best can witnesse.
Since then my Office hath so farre preuayl'd,
That Face to Face, and Royall Eye to Eye,
You haue congreeted: let it not disgrace me,
If I demand before this Royall view,
What Rub, or what Impediment there is,
Why that the naked, poore, and mangled Peace,
Deare Nourse of Arts, Plentyes, and ioyfull Births,
Should not in this best Garden of the World,
Our fertile France, put vp her louely Visage?
Alas, shee hath from France too long been chas'd,
And all her Husbandry doth lye on heapes,
Corrupting in it owne fertilitie.
Her Vine, the merry chearer of the heart,
Vnpruned, dyes: her Hedges euen pleach'd,
Like Prisoners wildly ouer-growne with hayre,
Put forth disorder'd Twigs: her fallow Leas,
The Darnell, Hemlock, and ranke Femetary,
Doth root vpon; while that the Culter rusts,

That should deracinate such Sauagery:
The euen Meade, that erst brought sweetly forth
The freckled Cowslip, Burnet, and greene Clouer,
Wanting the Sythe, withall vncorrected, ranke;
Conceiues by idlenesse, and nothing teemes,
But hatefull Docks, rough Thistles, Keksyes, Burres,
Loosing both beautie and vtilitie;
And all our Vineyards, Fallowes, Meades, and Hedges,
Defectiue in their natures, grow to wildnesse.
Euen so our Houses, and our selues, and Children,
Haue lost, or doe not learne, for want of time,
The Sciences that should become our Countrey;
But grow like Sauages, as Souldiers will,
That nothing doe, but meditate on Blood,
To Swearing, and sterne Lookes, defus'd Attyre,
And euery thing that seemes vnnaturall.
Which to reduce into our former fauour,
You are assembled: and my speech entreats,
That I may know the Let, why gentle Peace
Should not expell these inconueniences,
And blesse vs with her former qualities

Eng. If Duke of Burgonie, you would the Peace,
Whose want giues growth to th' imperfections
Which you haue cited; you must buy that Peace
With full accord to all our iust demands,
Whose Tenures and particular effects
You haue enschedul'd briefely in your hands

Burg. The King hath heard them: to the which, as yet
There is no Answer made

Eng. Well then: the Peace which you before so vrg'd,
Lyes in his Answer

France. I haue but with a curselarie eye
O're-glanc't the Articles: Pleaseth your Grace

To appoint some of your Councell presently
To sit with vs once more, with better heed
To re-suruey them; we will suddenly
Passe our accept and peremptorie Answer

England. Brother we shall. Goe Vnckle Exeter,
And Brother Clarence, and you Brother Gloucester,
Warwick, and Huntington, goe with the King,
And take with you free power, to ratifie,
Augment, or alter, as your Wisdomes best
Shall see aduantageable for our Dignitie,
Any thing in or out of our Demands,
And wee'le consigne thereto. Will you, faire Sister,
Goe with the Princes, or stay here with vs?
Quee. Our gracious Brother, I will goe with them:
Happily a Womans Voyce may doe some good,
When Articles too nicely vrg'd, be stood on

England. Yet leaue our Cousin Katherine here with vs,
She is our capitall Demand, compris'd
Within the fore-ranke of our Articles

Quee. She hath good leaue.

Exeunt. omnes.

Manet King and Katherine

King. Faire Katherine, and most faire,
Will you vouchsafe to teach a Souldier tearmes,
Such as will enter at a Ladyes eare,
And pleade his Loue-suit to her gentle heart

Kath. Your Maiestie shall mock at me, I cannot speake
your England

King. O faire Katherine, if you will loue me soundly with your
French heart, I will be glad to heare you confesse it brokenly
with your English Tongue. Doe you like me, Kate? Kath. Pardonne
moy, I cannot tell wat is like me

King. An Angell is like you Kate, and you are like an
Angell

Kath. Que dit il que Ie suis semblable a les Anges?
Lady. Ouy verayment (sauf vostre Grace) ainsi dit il

King. I said so, deare Katherine, and I must not blush
to affirme it

Kath. O bon Dieu, les langues des hommes sont plein de
tromperies

King. What sayes she, faire one? that the tongues of
men are full of deceits?
Lady. Ouy, dat de tongues of de mans is be full of deceits:
dat is de Princesse

King. The Princesse is the better English-woman: yfaith Kate, my
wooing is fit for thy vnderstanding, I am glad thou canst speake
no better English, for if thou could'st, thou would'st finde me
such a plaine King, that thou wouldst thinke, I had sold my
Farme to buy my Crowne. I know no wayes to mince it in loue,
but directly to say, I loue you; then if you vrge me farther, then
to say, Doe you in faith? I weare out my suite: Giue me your
answer, yfaith doe, and so clap hands, and a bargaine: how say
you, Lady? Kath. Sauf vostre honeur, me vnderstand well

King. Marry, if you would put me to Verses, or to Dance for your
sake, Kate, why you vndid me: for the one I haue neither words
nor measure; and for the other, I haue no strength in measure,
yet a reasonable measure in strength. If I could winne a Lady at
Leape-frogge, or by vawting into my Saddle, with my Armour on

my backe; vnder the correction of bragging be it spoken. I should quickly leape into a Wife: Or if I might buffet for my Loue, or bound my Horse for her fauours, I could lay on like a Butcher, and sit like a Iack an Apes, neuer off. But before God Kate, I cannot looke greenely, nor gaspe out my eloquence, nor I haue no cunning in protestation; onely downe-right Oathes, which I neuer vse till vrg'd, nor neuer breake for vrging. If thou canst loue a fellow of this temper, Kate, whose face is not worth Sunne-burning? that neuer lookes in his Glasse, for loue of any thing he sees there? let thine Eye be thy Cooke. I speake to thee plaine Souldier: If thou canst loue me for this, take me? if not? to say to thee that I shall dye, is true; but for thy loue, by the L[ord]. No: yet I loue thee too. And while thou liu'st, deare Kate, take a fellow of plaine and vncoyned Constancie, for he perforce must do thee right, because he hath not the gift to wooe in other places: for these fellowes of infinit tongue, that can ryme themselues into Ladyes fauours, they doe alwayes reason themselues out againe. What? a speaker is but a prater, a Ryme is but a Ballad; a good Legge will fall, a strait Backe will stoope, a blacke Beard will turne white, a curl'd Pate will grow bald, a faire Face will wither, a full Eye will wax hollow: but a good Heart, Kate, is the Sunne and the Moone, or rather the Sunne, and not the Moone; for it shines bright, and neuer changes, but keepes his course truly. If thou would haue such a one, take me? and take me; take a Souldier: take a Souldier; take a King. And what say'st thou then to my Loue? speake my faire, and fairely, I pray thee

Kath. Is it possible dat I sould loue de ennemie of Fraunce? King. No, it is not possible you should loue the Enemie of France, Kate; but in louing me, you should loue the Friend of France: for I loue France so well, that I will not part with a Village of it; I will haue it all mine: and Kate, when France is mine, and I am yours; then yours is France, and you are mine

Kath. I cannot tell wat is dat

King. No, Kate? I will tell thee in French, which I am sure will
hang vpon my tongue, like a new-married Wife about her
Husbands Necke, hardly to be shooke off; Ie quand sur le
possession de Fraunce, & quand vous aues le possession de moy.
(Let mee see, what then? Saint Dennis bee my speede) Donc
vostre est Fraunce, & vous estes mienne. It is as easie for me,
Kate, to conquer the Kingdome, as to speake so much more
French: I shall neuer moue thee in French, vnlesse it be to laugh
at me

Kath. Sauf vostre honeur, le Francois ques vous parleis, il &
melieus que l' Anglois le quel Ie parle

King. No faith is't not, Kate: but thy speaking of my Tongue, and I
thine, most truely falsely, must needes be graunted to be much
at one. But Kate, doo'st thou vnderstand thus much English?
Canst thou loue mee? Kath. I cannot tell

King. Can any of your Neighbours tell, Kate? Ile aske them. Come,
I know thou louest me: and at night, when you come into your
Closet, you'le question this Gentlewoman about me; and I know,
Kate, you will to her disprayse those parts in me, that you loue
with your heart: but good Kate, mocke me mercifully, the rather
gentle Princesse, because I loue thee cruelly. If euer thou beest
mine, Kate, as I haue a sauing Faith within me tells me thou
shalt; I get thee with skambling, and thou must therefore needes
proue a good Souldier-breeder: Shall not thou and I, betweene
Saint Dennis and Saint George, compound a Boy, halfe French
halfe English, that shall goe to Constantinople, and take the
Turke by the Beard. Shall wee not? what say'st thou, my faire
Flower-de-Luce

Kate. I doe not know dat

King. No: 'tis hereafter to know, but now to promise: doe but
now promise Kate, you will endeauour for your French part of
such a Boy; and for my English moytie, take the Word of a King,

and a Batcheler. How answer you. La plus belle Katherine du
monde mon trescher & deuin deesse

Kath. Your Maiestee aue fause Frenche enough to deceiue de
most sage Damoiseil dat is en Fraunce

King. Now fye vpon my false French: by mine Honor in true
English, I loue thee Kate; by which Honor, I dare not sweare thou
louest me, yet my blood begins to flatter me, that thou doo'st;
notwithstanding the poore and vntempering effect of my Visage.
Now beshrew my Fathers Ambition, hee was thinking of Ciuill
Warres when hee got me, therefore was I created with a
stubborne out-side, with an aspect of Iron, that when I come to
wooe Ladyes, I fright them: but in faith Kate, the elder I wax, the
better I shall appeare. My comfort is, that Old Age, that ill layer
vp of Beautie, can doe no more spoyle vpon my Face. Thou hast
me, if thou hast me, at the worst; and thou shalt weare me, if
thou weare me, better and better: and therefore tell me, most
faire Katherine, will you haue me? Put off your Maiden Blushes,
auouch the Thoughts of your Heart with the Lookes of an
Empresse, take me by the Hand, and say, Harry of England, I am
thine: which Word thou shalt no sooner blesse mine Eare withall,
but I will tell thee alowd, England is thine, Ireland is thine,
France is thine, and Henry Plantaginet is thine; who, though I
speake it before his Face, if he be not Fellow with the best King,
thou shalt finde the best King of Good-fellowes. Come your
Answer in broken Musick; for thy Voyce is Musick, and thy
English broken: Therefore Queene of all, Katherine, breake thy
minde to me in broken English; wilt thou haue me? Kath. Dat is
as it shall please de Roy mon pere

King. Nay, it will please him well, Kate; it shall please him, Kate

Kath. Den it sall also content me

King. Vpon that I kisse your Hand, and I call you my
Queene

Kath. Laisse mon Seigneur, laisse, laisse, may foy: Ie ne veus point que vous abbaisse vostre grandeus, en baisant le main d' une nostre Seigneur indignie seruiteur excuse moy. Ie vous supplie mon tres-puissant Seigneur

King. Then I will kisse your Lippes, Kate

Kath. Les Dames & Damoisels pour estre baisee deuant leur nopcese il net pas le costume de Fraunce

King. Madame, my Interpreter, what sayes shee?
Lady. Dat it is not be de fashon pour le Ladies of Fraunce; I cannot tell wat is buisse en Anglish

King. To kisse

Lady. Your Maiestee entendre bettre que moy

King. It is not a fashion for the Maids in Fraunce to kisse before they are marryed, would she say?
Lady. Ouy verayment

King. O Kate, nice Customes cursie to great Kings. Deare Kate, you and I cannot bee confin'd within the weake Lyst of a Countreyes fashion: wee are the makers of Manners, Kate; and the libertie that followes our Places, stoppes the mouth of all finde-faults, as I will doe yours, for vpholding the nice fashion of your Countrey, in denying me a Kisse: therefore patiently, and yeelding. You haue Witch-craft in your Lippes, Kate: there is more eloquence in a Sugar touch of them, then in the Tongues of the French Councell; and they should sooner perswade Harry of England, then a generall Petition of Monarchs. Heere comes your Father.
Enter the French Power, and the English Lords.

Burg. God saue your Maiestie, my Royall Cousin, teach you our Princesse English?

King. I would haue her learne, my faire Cousin, how
perfectly I loue her, and that is good English

Burg. Is shee not apt? King. Our Tongue is rough, Coze, and my
Condition is not smooth: so that hauing neyther the Voyce nor
the Heart of Flatterie about me, I cannot so coniure vp the Spirit
of Loue in her, that hee will appeare in his true likenesse

Burg. Pardon the franknesse of my mirth, if I answer you for
that. If you would coniure in her, you must make a Circle: if
coniure vp Loue in her in his true likenesse, hee must appeare
naked, and blinde. Can you blame her then, being a Maid, yet
ros'd ouer with the Virgin Crimson of Modestie, if shee deny the
apparance of a naked blinde Boy in her naked seeing selfe? It
were (my Lord) a hard Condition for a Maid to consigne to

King. Yet they doe winke and yeeld, as Loue is blind
and enforces

Burg. They are then excus'd, my Lord, when they see
not what they doe

King. Then good my Lord, teach your Cousin to
consent winking

Burg. I will winke on her to consent, my Lord, if you will teach
her to know my meaning: for Maides well Summer'd, and warme
kept, are like Flyes at Bartholomew-tyde, blinde, though they
haue their eyes, and then they will endure handling, which
before would not abide looking on

King. This Morall tyes me ouer to Time, and a hot Summer; and
so I shall catch the Flye, your Cousin, in the latter end, and she
must be blinde to

Burg. As Loue is my Lord, before it loues

King. It is so: and you may, some of you, thanke
Loue for my blindnesse, who cannot see many a faire
French Citie for one faire French Maid that stands in my
way

French King. Yes my Lord, you see them perspectiuely: the Cities
turn'd into a Maid; for they are all gyrdled with Maiden Walls,
that Warre hath entred

England. Shall Kate be my Wife?
France. So please you

England. I am content, so the Maiden Cities you talke of, may
wait on her: so the Maid that stood in the way for my Wish, shall
shew me the way to my Will

France. Wee haue consented to all tearmes of reason

England. Is't so, my Lords of England?
West. The King hath graunted euery Article:
His Daughter first; and in sequele, all,
According to their firme proposed natures

Exet. Onely he hath not yet subscribed this: Where your Maiestie
demands, That the King of France hauing any occasion to write
for matter of Graunt, shall name your Highnesse in this forme,
and with this addition, in French: Nostre trescher filz Henry Roy
d' Angleterre Heretere de Fraunce: and thus in Latine;
Praeclarissimus Filius noster Henricus Rex Angliæ & Heres
Franciae

France. Nor this I haue not Brother so deny'd,
But your request shall make me let it passe

England. I pray you then, in loue and deare allyance,
Let that one Article ranke with the rest,
And thereupon giue me your Daughter

109

France. Take her faire Sonne, and from her blood rayse vp
Issue to me, that the contending Kingdomes
Of France and England, whose very shoares looke pale,
With enuy of each others happinesse,
May cease their hatred; and this deare Coniunction
Plant Neighbour-hood and Christian-like accord
In their sweet Bosomes: that neuer Warre aduance
His bleeding Sword 'twixt England and faire France

Lords. Amen

King. Now welcome Kate: and beare me witnesse all,
That here I kisse her as my Soueraigne Queene.

Flourish.

Quee. God, the best maker of all Marriages,
Combine your hearts in one, your Realmes in one:
As Man and Wife being two, are one in loue,
So be there 'twixt your Kingdomes such a Spousall,
That neuer may ill Office, or fell Iealousie,
Which troubles oft the Bed of blessed Marriage,
Thrust in betweene the Paction of these Kingdomes,
To make diuorce of their incorporate League:
That English may as French, French Englishmen,
Receiue each other. God speake this Amen

All. Amen

King. Prepare we for our Marriage: on which day,
My Lord of Burgundy wee'le take your Oath
And all the Peeres, for suretie of our Leagues.
Then shall I sweare to Kate, and you to me,
And may our Oathes well kept and prosp'rous be.

Senet. Exeunt.

Enter Chorus.

Thus farre with rough, and all-vnable Pen,
Our bending Author hath pursu'd the Story,
In little roome confining mightie men,
Mangling by starts the full course of their glory.
Small time: but in that small, most greatly liued
This Starre of England. Fortune made his Sword;
By which, the Worlds best Garden he atchieued:
And of it left his Sonne Imperiall Lord.
Henry the Sixt, in Infant Bands crown'd King
Of France and England, did this King succeed:
Whose State so many had the managing,
That they lost France, and made his England bleed:
Which oft our Stage hath showne; and for their sake,
In your faire minds let this acceptance take.

Made in the USA
Lexington, KY
20 April 2015